PRAISE FOR KING'S HIGHWAY

King's Highway **is a journey not easily forgotten.**
    ~ Carla Damron, *The Stone Necklace*

A coming-of-age story that any teenager, especially one who grew up in South Carolina, **will recognize in some way as his or her own story.**
    ~ Robert Lamb, *Striking Out* and *Atlanta Blues*

King's Highway provides **the perfect literary scrapbook to relive a bygone era.**
    ~Robbie Robertson, *Grand Strand Magazine*

The author **hits the bullseye** with his main character, Myrtle Beach itself... what it felt like **when we thought the fun would never end**, and what it felt like when it finally did.
    ~Ben Steelman, *Wilmington Star-News*

King's Highway is a wonderfully written first novel by James D. McCallister, who brings to life a bygone era on the Grand Strand. **This should be required summer reading!**
    ~ Karen Petit, the *Shandon's Ivy League Mystery Series*

James D. McCallister has given us a cleverly constructed, compelling story... **McCallister's witty, unhurried style makes this book a winner.**
    ~ Bert Goolsby, *Her Own Law* and *Harpers' Joy*

King's Highway

King's Highway

JAMES D. McCALLISTER

MHP
Mind Harvest Press
COLUMBIA, SC

ISBN: 978-1-946052-08-7 (ppbk); 978-1-946052-09-4 (ebook)

Library of Congress: 2018911594

For more information:

Mind Harvest Press
COLUMBIA, SC

Mind Harvest Press
PO Box 50552
Columbia SC 29250-0552
www.jamesdmccallister.com

CONTENTS

For Eddie

It is an illusion that youth is happy, an illusion of those who have lost it; but the young know they are wretched for they are full of the truthless ideals which have been instilled into them, and each time they come in contact with the real, they are bruised and wounded.

—Somerset Maugham

1

JOHNNY STRIKES UP THE BAND

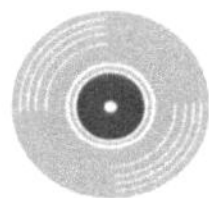

Ever had one of those dreams where you're trying to scream, but you have no voice? Well, that's the way my life seems to me in the spring of 1978, in the winter of my nineteenth year. I traipse around the campus of venerable Southeastern University pretending to be an engaged student of the world; I should be coming into my own. I should be discovering the *me* inside me. But rather than finding direction, nurturing ambition, and realizing potential—growing up, in other words —instead I drift sideward on a desultory, turbid sea of uncertainty.

I am a message in a bottle. For the life of me, though, I don't know what the note inside says.

Oh, to an outsider I'm sure my life of privilege must seem peachy-keen, and in a sense it is—unlike some folks these days, the DeKalbs are doing all right indeed. My brother and I want for nothing. We are princes. We are Americans. Life is good.

For me, however, this time of plenty comes at what seems a dreadful price: In the DeKalb household, you see, free will is a precious commodity.

I have no voice, yet I must scream.

A further complication may be that, even if I were to find my one and true voice, I don't know if I have anything to say. If I, Raymond DeKalb, have such a voice, it is subsumed not only within my father's carefully laid out plans for my future, but also by the many other voices I'm able to produce in the service of amusement for my fellow humans. The one talent I seem to possess is my ability to mimic anyone and anything (well, with a little practice), but none of these vocal affectations represent anything close to the real me.

The voices, the voices. They allow me to hide. They keep the rest of the world at arm's length. I feel like John Travolta in that bubble-boy TV movie—trapped by circumstance, unable to connect with anyone, hermetically sealed off.

I endure the urgent calling to find out who I am and what else there is of the world besides the podunk Carolina town that has thus far been my home, as well as the great and vast state university at which I am but one of thousands just-like-me. As young men are wont to do in such moments of sensual and intellectual yearning, I seek to explore, to break free, to find myself, perhaps, by losing myself. But how? And to where shall I roam? For now, my intellectual wanderings are but in a circle.

●

I REMEMBER how I felt the first time I ever went anywhere without the rest of my family, which was to a burgeoning tourist trap on the coast called Myrtle Beach, for a week of relaxation and celebration not only of graduation from Marion Sims High School, but also my impending matriculation at summer's end to the universe of higher learning. With my compatriots in youthful abandon, I made what is around these parts a fairly traditional journey—after commencement, you and your friends pile into someone's car and haul butt down to Sun Fun week, at which point you all begin to party like there's no tomorrow.

Did I come back enlightened in any way? Not exactly—more like hungover, sated, in a sense, on excess. However:

I felt liberated and alive at finally being away from my family and our comfortable home in Tillman Falls, a picture-postcard Southern small town if there ever was one: Old money, horse country, filled with a genteel but arrogant populace of souls still metaphorically fighting the War of Northern Aggression even these hundred-plus years later, with attitudes of intolerance lingering like the fart-stink of collard greens simmering in

Pitty Pat's kitchen. They are my people, yes—they are all I've ever known —but I feel like a stranger there. Always have.

Even though I am a lifelong South Carolinian, prior to that Sun Fun trip, I'd never set foot in Myrtle Beach. My family has always vacationed either at our lake house, or else on Edisto or maybe Hilton Head Island, at the southern end of the state's shoreline—that's where the well-to-do people go. There are movie stars and rock stars and politicians and the like on a place like Hilton Head, but the DeKalbs aren't rock stars—far from it, as a matter of fact. My dad's a quasi-hot shot, small town Southern lawyer who is gearing up to run for the State House in the fall. Someone of his class wouldn't deign to vacation in a garish, proletarian environment like the Grand Strand, as they call it. No, no, the DeKalbs are too good for that. Which is why, I think, I loved it so while I was there on Ocean Boulevard. Felt like freedom, a vacation not from work, but from my life as I had heretofore known it.

At Myrtle Beach, I could be whomever I wanted. And it was this feeling to which I wanted to return, wherever I could find it.

⚬

RICHARD DEKALB'S modest fortune doesn't only come from the lawyer game: Dad and his buddies are heavily into playing the stock market, and to hear him boast about it, they're making money hand over fist, even though the economy is really in the tank thanks to Carter and the oil sheiks—again, to hear him tell it.

I wonder, sometimes, if we have as much money as he lets on. Behind closed doors, he does a lot of nit-picky complaining about what things cost. To the outside world, though, you'd think he was Marvin Mitchell or some other big-time, famous lawyer. You got to sell it, he tells me. You got to sell it to the people if you want to get something back. I think he's full of shit, and sometimes I even tell him so, but, boy howdy, does he not appreciate that particular sentiment, not one bit.

I wonder if the problems we have in this country go back a long time before Carter, but I'm just a kid so what do I know? My earliest memories of politics revolve around Vietnam (blood and guts on the evening news) and Watergate (viscera of a different, more inscrutable sort).

Easy, perhaps, to blame our gentle Christian president for problems that have festered for longer, perhaps, than our country has even been around. Probably too nice for politics, this James Earl Carter. One wonders if, on some days, he thinks maybe he should have stayed on the peanut farm.

Nothing gentle about the elder Mr. DeKalb, though: Daddy's an ambitious, loud, barrel-chested man who has entered middle age, the "prime of life" as he reminds me constantly, and he's going places. Now that the school board is too small potatoes for him, he really seems hip to go to Columbia and be a big-time state politician, running for the seat to be soon vacated by a long-lived political legend here in our district named Lonnie Allen Sheehan, who has become too old and too sick to go on. To hear Dad and his brethren boast about it, there's no chance he won't win. Whoop-tee-doo. I find it all rather distasteful.

But my mom? She'll love that kind of gig. She loves to socialize and throw parties and let people know they (we) have some money. She is all about appearances. Presenting Mr. Richard DeKalb, and his lovely and capable wife, Ruth. Now see: Their two fine sons, Jenkins (a family name on Ruth's side) and little Ray-Ray, both handsome young college men, chips off the old block, and following in the old man's footsteps whether they want to or not. (Hint: Jenkins wants to be Daddy as badly as I do not, so you'd think that would be enough for the crusty old bastard. Apparently not, though.)

I don't care about the money part so much. Really.

Oh, hell, who am I kidding? That bread is what keeps me in dope and LPs and books right now, in addition to paying for the car, tuition, food, clothing—you know the drill. But I definitely don't have much interest in the school board, or being a state senator, or being the President of the goddamn United States either.

And furthermore, I don't trust anyone who would want to be any of those things. The way I feel about politics (and Daddy's world in general) is like a combination of *Catch-22* and that Groucho Marx joke Woody Allen borrowed for *Annie Hall*: You can't be crazy if you don't want to fly any more missions because you'd have to be crazy to *want* to fly more missions, and any club that would admit someone like me—or my father —as a member is a suspicious organization indeed. If that sounds convoluted, I bet you still get what I'm trying to say. Hey—I said right from the git-go I was mixed up, didn't I?

·

THIS WAS the latest scene wherein I attempted to explain to Daddy how I'm not on board with his little scheme for me and my future, and I thought I'd rather be, oh, a teacher, or a social worker, helping people somehow—living a meaningful life, in other words.

After my heartfelt oration he replied, apoplectic and nearly swooning with annoyance: "Son: you've got to think about the future. I mean, *seriously*, now. I thought we all agreed—y'all got to let me run at least *one* of my boys for governor some day. Jenkins is fine, he gonna be a fine lawyer soon enough." He dropped his voice. "But you're a lot smarter than him."

"No disagreement there."

"Ain't nobody ever heard of a goddurn social worker who become Governor of South Carolina. You heard of one, boy?"

I ignored him and soldiered on: "I also thought about the Peace Corps for a couple years after I get done at Southeastern. This grad student I met, she went to Belize, or someplace in Central America, said it was good. Helping those people, I mean. Said she experienced personal growth." I didn't really mean any of it—I knew such talk would give him a hard-on, and not the good kind.

Dear old Dad, apparently not listening very well: "Following some girl around? That's so silly. Central *America*. Silly-silly. Get your feet on the ground!"

Silly-silly. Just like the way they've always called me Ray-Ray. Silly-silly little Ray-Ray. In the end, I walked away like always, letting him think he'd won another round. I was boiling inside, though. Boiling.

Why can't the old man be satisfied with Jenkins, who is apparently quite eager to follow Daddy's plan to the letter—hell, my brother's probably already rehearsing the inauguration day speech he'll give one day down on the granite steps of the State House. Jenkins is way, way on board with all that—except Jenkins is *not* the old man, except perhaps in body-type. Like our astute patriarch said, my older brother doesn't have the smarts, only the ambition. Oh, well, I guess he's smart enough. But you don't have to be a genius to get into law school, after all—I grew up around Daddy and his buddies, and none of them have ever seemed to be world-beaters in the brains department.

Jenkins. He's a chubby little lazybones, that boy, and worse, he's a light in his loafers, typical Tillman Falls rich preppie boy, with his khaki pants and penny-loafers and mannerly drawl. I've worked hard through the years to rid myself of the twang, which probably helps explain all the other asinine voices I do.

My brother's had everything handed to him, and I don't think he understands about having to work for personal gain. (I don't either, by the way.) Jenkins is not like his daddy in that regard. Dick DeKalb is a hard worker, anything but lazy. Jenkins DeKalb is to Richard DeKalb like a pencil tracing is to an oil painting. Jenkins is like the bones without the meat. Jenkins is a pale shadow. He's a smart-mouth know-it-all, and I can't fucking stand him. He'll go on expecting everything to be given to him, for the rest of his life—and the worst part? He'll probably get it.

As for me, three weeks into the spring semester of my sophomore year at big old Southeastern I find myself dying inside. I don't know anymore whether I want to shit or go blind. Even though I thought I had an idea at one time of what direction to take, I realize now I don't want to be a teacher, or a social worker, or a scientist, or an astronaut (tee-hee), or anything else you can imagine me becoming. All I know is that I do not wish to be a part of the nascent DeKalb Political Dynasty here in South Carolina—Daddy's carefully cultivated notion that, a generation down the line, we'll become the Kennedys of the south, permanently decamped to Hilton Head as though it were the redneck version of Martha's Vineyard. Sounds like an untenable crock of bullcrap to me.

And lest you think I am being melodramatic, consider this actual snippet of dialog from Richard DeKalb, Esquire, one night when he had had one Dickel and Sprite too many: "Think of it fellas, Attorney General Raymond DeKalb. Governor," he paused, his eyes watering, "*Governor* Jenkins DeKalb. It gives me the cold chills, I tell you." He shuddered. "Senator DeKalb. Secretary DeKalb…it gives me cold chills."

"Well, shoot, Daddy, why c'ain't I be the *gub'ner*?" I said this with a small smile and an exaggerated low country drawl, as though Ernest Hollings and I had just arrived, clip-clopping underneath the portico in a horse-drawn surrey. "And I shore as heck don't want to be no one's *se*cretary, for heaven's sake."

"Well, son. There's no reason you can't. No sir. Both boys becoming governor? Lord have *mercy*. What a legacy."

Now I'd done it.

Jenkins snorted. "Shut up, Ray-Ray. You don't even want to go to law school. If you ask me, what you want to do is some hippy-dippy, pussy-ass shit. And you can go off and do it, for all we care. Right, Daddy?"

"Now, son. I hardly think such remarks will inspire Ray-Ray here to—"

"No, I'm serious. Didn't you tell me Ray wants to go help the blacks in Africa, or some nonsense? Well, I think we ought to let him. To build character, helping our tan cousins erect their huts and tote their river-water."

They both snickered, well-off white men with stomachs straining in a valiant effort to pop the buttons on their oxford shirts, while I suffered a hot flush rising in my cheeks. That kind of talk pisses me off. I've worked hard to shake off those old Jim Crow attitudes, like I've tried to kill the corn-pone accent. This is 1978, for pity's sake. Dr. King gave his life to combat the notions these men find so amusing.

In any case, Jenkins is way on board, well on his way to being the next Pitchfork Ben Tillman here in SC like dear old Dad wants. And that's going to have to be enough. I mean, Jenkins's already been a House page in D.C., and swears he nailed a genuine U.S. Representative's daughter, that of Crom Burtwell, R-Georgia, daughter's name Courtney; Jenkins claims in his crude manner how he "did" her right on the congressman's own desk. Somehow I'm certain my brother's off on the right foot to become a politician.

As an undergrad at Southeastern, my esteemed sibling also has more wholesome entries on his CV: wrote a well-received, conservative political column in the *Redtails Review*, though in all honesty it was only admired by his own breed, and was roundly and consistently lambasted by the more liberal elements on campus. Jenkins is the kind of guy who thinks Ronald Reagan, a has-been movie actor, ought to be president—in other words, he's got a screw loose. The DeKalbs have been Democrats for as long as there have been Democrats. But times change, and polarities shift between pendulums.

What will be my part in this great family political saga? Am I to be a third-rate Billy Carter? Or else, a more important role?

How about changing my name so no one knows I have a connection to this bunch of freaks? That'd be a good start.

Oh, I'm being melodramatic. I guess the family is not that bad. I don't feel like I belong, though. Ever get that feeling? Well, now, I tell you, I gots it bad, suffering through this ridiculous semester, one in which I have taken the Intro to Journalism class as a way of sampling that profession.

Yes, I am thinking about switching majors—again. Maybe teaching isn't the answer. Maybe a career as a member of the fourth estate, reporting on the state of the world to the rest of civilization, trying to get at some semblance of truth about our mutual, universal human condition.

Truth, eh?

The truth is, I am lost.

Not lost like a dog that has gotten loose, but lost like a plane-crashed group of soccer players on the top of an Andean mountain. And the problem is, I don't want to get to the point where I am so lost, so hopelessly fucked, that I start to eat my own flesh.

I can't believe I will be twenty at year's end—I feel an acute pang, the loss of childhood, in these moments, when I must acknowledge I am no longer a kid, and yet I don't know who I am as an adult. I feel in-between, out of sorts, a bit player about to make an entrance onto the stage in the middle of a play he's never read. I feel cowed and intimidated by people who ought to be my peers. I hide behind humor and sarcasm because I don't really know how to relate to anyone. But I want to learn.

No, I am *desperate* to learn. But how?

●

SO MY ROOMMATE Chris and I discuss this and other subjects at length one night, passing the bong back and forth in our generic little apartment a few blocks from campus over on Sugeree Street, in a 1940s-era duplex, drafty and prone to insect infestation—but hey, it's home, I guess.

We became friends in English 101, and moved out of the dorms together last fall (against the strenuous objections of my worry-wart mother). Chris is a musician, and wants to teach music to kids, God love him, in addition to being the front man of his little new-wave rock band. His head isn't in the clouds, though: He knows he won't be the next Whomever and the Whoevers, topping the charts, nailing models and cashing royalty checks and all that overly glamorized whatnot. Chris feels he can get what he needs out of life by teaching others to see what's cool about the stuff that gets him off—hell, he's already making some nice bread teaching guitar-god licks to adolescent boys. I envy his sense of self, at times, to the point of resentment.

Listen to this twerp: "I like making music. I respond when I see other people stimulated and interested in music. If I can shepherd someone along in that direction, then it's good for me and for them. And for the whole world, I think. If that's all I ever do—help one kid realize his musical dreams—that'll be enough."

Chris is something of a philosopher as well as an accomplished guitarist, and fancies himself an intellectual. He's from Florida by way of New England, and came to Southeastern because of some famous classical musician who teaches here. He's good looking and gets lots of girls—but musicians always do, don't they?

He goes on: "Art, you see, is the greatest act man can do with his time here on earth, the highest expression of the divinity, if you will, within us all. Music, poetry, painting, acting, writing—to not only do it, but inspire others to seek out the expression of their own truth."

"And the worst man can do with his time?"

"Warfare, I guess." A long pause. Smoke, wafting. "Abject cruelty, in whatever form it might take. Moral turpitude—confidence men who prey on the elderly. Pederasts, murderers. Liars. Thieves. Politicians," concluding with disdain.

"You covered a lot of ground with that last one, man."

"Lot of ground to be covered."

Chris does the stoner drift-away, humming to himself, a musician composing in his head, I suppose. He's so smart. I'm always surprised when it's left to me to keep the conversation going. "But yeah—art and warfare. There's a real polarity to the ideas. Creation and destruction."

He smacks his lips, suffers a crackling case of cotton-mouth. "Can there ever be earthly justice for monsters like Nixon and Kissinger?"

"Mass murderers. Millions dead."

"That's what I mean."

"A new Nuremberg trial? Where? By whom? Who by?"

"Never happen."

"That's what I'm saying."

But what about me and my problems? Chris says of these existential matters, "I think that you need to look within. Pull it inside, poke around in there. Yes: The answer is within. You have to find it, to flush it out from its hiding place. That which you seek is already there, bro. Flush it out like a rabbit from the underbrush."

I take a giant hit off the bong, release the smoke slowly through my next words. "I think that I'm reaching some weird point where all I know is what I *don't* want." Holding the filthy ceramic tube in my right hand, a curl of smoke creeping from the opening in the top, I put the bong down and prop up my dingy Chuck Taylors on the rough-hewn wooden coffee table, really just a big crate covered in magazines, dope seeds and scraps of notebook paper. "I don't know what to look for, only what to avoid. That's no way to live."

"What are these things you want to avoid? The unacceptable pathways among your choices, so to speak?" Chris already sounds like a professor. Sometimes I think he tries too hard, though, mainly to impress girls, but also to impress me and everyone else as well. I'm no slouch—I've been a big reader since I was a kid, and at one time I even thought about writing, but when I tried, damned if I had anything to say.

"Dad's got his head up his ass if he still thinks I'm going to law school. That's a key issue here. *The* issue."

"Law school—*ugh*," he says with scorn. "It's the lowest."

"That's the way I feel."

"Your father, based upon the description you've offered to me in the past, will be somewhat unforgiving of your newfound contumacy."

"My *what?*"

"Your apostate status within the DeKalb family."

"*Huh?*"

"That you're about to tell him to go fuck himself about all the lawyer-talk," he exclaims. "Sheesh."

We both laugh. I was only playing dumb anyway.

"You're right. It won't be easy. They won't understand. How do you say, 'Dad, everything I have been, and all you—my folks—wish me to become, none of this holds any interest for me anymore, if it ever did in the first place?' It's the only thing I'm certain about, but to them, it's beyond unacceptable."

"It's sweet of you to consider their feelings."

I never thought about it. It's family. It's what you do. "But what about my feelings? That's the problem."

"Well-then," he concludes. "You'll have to do some looking outside of yourself too, I guess. One cannot choose a path unless he can see the choices in front of him. Look within first, then without."

"Maybe I'll try to do both at once, look within—"

"—as well as without. Good. *Good.*"

The *perfessor* nods with approval. I admire Chris, while at the same time suffer in annoyance at observing someone who has his shit wired so straight. Studious little buttholes like Chris, so good at everything, so poised, so wise, so confident. Fuck him and his pedantic shit.

But it continues unabated: "So listen, there's this new album by a talented songwriter I've just discovered. I want you to hear it—nay, I *insist*. It is chock-full of great little insidious pop songs. It is just the cat's meow. Seriously. Short and sweet. Thirty-one minutes and done. I am in envious awe of this gentleman."

"What is it?" I look at the cover of the record by this cat named Warren Zevon. He appears impish, insouciant, self-assured. His music, singer-songwriter poetry set to catchy rock guitar hooks, speaks to me from the first notes.

◦

THE NEXT DAY I'm cruising around campus, completely stoned and totally blowing off every class I've got, and I start thinking about the whole within/without deal, and I get all bunched up inside. Tight and bothersome. Like I can barely breathe.

Dizzy, I ease down onto a bench on the Pinckney Street overpass, and consider the possibility of starting smoking cigarettes again, a brief affectation from my senior year back at Sims High. My nylon book bag sits slumped at my feet like a sad sack of rotten potatoes, a burgundy lump of nothing, the books and notebooks inside as useless to me as a sledge-hammer to a brain surgeon.

Then: a real bummer.

Who should come dilly-boppin' up the way but my ex-girlfriend, Nola-Marie Stimson, of the Tillman Falls Stimsons, high school sweetheart, first love, all that jive. I want to say being dumped by her was a good thing, but I still can't yet. My self-confidence is still low. I haven't even hooked up with anyone else yet, and it's been months, since before Christmas. She looks pretty damn good—she's the only woman with whom I've made humpty-hump, which is no small thing.

With her un-tucked blue oxford shirt, black pedal-pushers and white Keds, she either seems deliriously out of style, or perhaps ahead of her time, or *something*. She's pretty in that small-Southern-town kind of way, with a conservative little hair bob and fairly traditional makeup, but just sophisticated enough to want to be a touch artier than all that, especially since she's at Southeastern now. She wants to impress people, make sure they know she's hip and all—even if she, in reality, is far from it: Another small-town small-timer like me. The oxford shirt, though, probably serves more to obscure a too-voluptuous figure than it does to make any sort of fashion statement, either mainstream or alternative.

"Well, hey there," she says, all sweet and friendly. "You finally decide to go to class?"

"And regretting it, now."

A flicker of sadness in her eyes. "Aw."

"I'm surprised to see you out in the daylight," my attempt at a savage, bitter insult, the first of several. "Since when do they let you animals walk around, out in the open? The zoo-keepers, I mean?"

"Insults? That's all you have to say?"

I switch to my late grandmother's thick patois. "Oh, my lord—when are you having electrolysis on that *mole*, Nola? It looks just awful. And you got a white bump on your nose. You oughta *pop* it, girl. Mercy me—you just a mess."

"Why must you be this way?" One hand on her ample hip, the other holding the left strap of her own nylon book bag, she cuts a figure of undeniable appeal. I ache at the memory of once having my hand on that hip, holding on, so to speak. "I don't see why we can't just be friends. Do you know what animosity means?"

"You caused this."

"Do you know about forgiveness? Do you remember from Sunday school?"

"I quit going when I was twelve."

"You used to come to events at church with me, though. When we were together. The youth group."

I laugh with derision. "I was stoned every time I went to that shit with you. Didn't you realize?"

Her sarcastic, annoyed half-smile fades into a full on frown. "No."

"All I cared about," I say, rising off the bench, "was getting into those knickers of yours. But it's not like there ain't plenty more around." I do a Mick Jagger funky-chicken strut back and forth in front of her. "You think you're the only girl in town? *Well, you ain't.*"

"That's awful, Ray. It's not fair."

Feeling foolish, I stop dancing. "Well, neither was what you did to me."

"Oh, grow up. People change."

"No, *you* grow up," I reply in a petulant, high shriek. Another silly voice.

"Just forget it." She starts to stomp off in a huff, but stops. Over her shoulder, smug: "You better be nice to me. We need to—well. We should try and be friends. I said I was sorry, and these things happen."

"Why?"

"I—I can't help my feelings. Anyway, you just better try harder," she says with a weird, self-righteous look before hurrying down the steps toward the old campus.

I wonder what it all means and try to forget about feeling betrayed by someone I didn't really love in the first place. In time, I'm quite sure I would have broken up with her anyway, but the fact that she did it to me was so excruciating and annoying I've been unable to let it go. I almost want to get some kind of a spite-fuck out of it, honestly. But that would probably cause more problems than it would solve, really. No doubt.

The thought of such a tryst, instilled with malice rather than passion, gives me a shudder of creepily erotic fervor. I feel icky, and try to shake off the weirdness.

Okay: Seeing Nola-Marie is the last fucking straw, a signpost toward the future and not the past.

I must act.

*

I MARCH straight over to Sugeree Street and explain to my roommate how I want to drop out of school and go live somewhere else for a while. This revelation, which came to me in a flash as I studied Nola's retreating posterior region, seems disturbing to Chris.

"Are you kidding? What the hell for?"

"Hell, no I ain't kiddin', beau." I offer this in a thick redneck accent which turns threatening. *"Do I look like I'm a-funnin' you, boy?"*

"But seriously," Chris says. "You can't be serious."

"Ain't kidding," in my own voice.

Arms folded in disapproval. "You have a lease on this stupid apartment with me until August, you little butthole." Chris comes from a single-parent household of modest means; his father died tragically when his only son was but a lad of nine. "Who's going to pay your half of every-thing? I'm on my own, remember?"

I try to explain in no uncertain terms how I'd see what I could do about that part of it. "Besides, if nothing works out, I mean—I'll be back here. I reckon."

"Maybe you will."

"Huh?"

"After making such a big decision, who knows where life will take you."

"In any case, I won't leave you on the hook." I have a small trust fund from my grandfather who left us some scratch when he died a couple of years ago, but I only get a small stipend once a month until the age of twenty-five. Nothing much to speak of, but a smidgen of free money. "If you can't find a tenant, I'll slip you some bucks."

"What, through the mail?"

"Sure. From wherever I end up."

"That'll be the day."

Chris and I slip back into philosophical mode, spending twenty minutes grinding through another rigorous session of assessment regarding my ruinous ennui, until the phone rings and interrupts the dialogue. It's my cousin Kenny-Ken. Still only a senior in high school, he's leagues ahead in knowing what he wants to do with himself: He's a movie nut and is planning to, like, go off to Hollywood. He's actually made little super-8 films and all! No shit. He's the kind of kid who asks for a subscription to *Variety* as a Christmas gift.

I call him Kenny-Ken because he sort of changed from Kenny to Ken in the last year or so, feeling that "Kenny"—his mother's, and my aunt's, preferred moniker for her only baby—was somehow belittling to a budding auteur about to explode onto the Hollywood scene. Kenny is a little boy, but "Ken," on the hand, now that sounds like a hip grownup dude. Companion to Barbie, and all. A cultural touchstone.

"Hey, what's going on, Kenny-Ken?" I realize addressing him as such is my way of denigrating my younger cousin, like the way I feel when my family does the whole Ray-Ray bit. My self-awareness in this moment is staggering—gratifying, even.

"*Bro.* Come on with that shit."

"You got it, Kenny-Ken." Taunt, wicked laughter. And since he's family, I can't help but slip into Edgewater County Bubba voice: "What can I do you for, beau?"

"I need to—uh—to come see ya."

From his inflection, I know what he wants: Weed.

It figures. Tillman Falls isn't exactly the bud capital of the world, but, man, this campus has plenty. Do I have time for this sort of foolishness, though? "I don't know if I can help you out right now, man."

"Been dry over there too?"

It hadn't, but having bigger fish to fry, I feel like neither sharing nor procuring smokeable commodities right now. Doesn't he realize I'm having existential problems?

But a friend, a cousin, in need, here: "I reckon I can call around. It shouldn't be a problem."

He's relieved. "*Cool.* I'll come over later. We'll hang out. Thanks, man."

Click.

If I can't find any herb for Kenny-Ken, Chris offers to throw me a bud or two out of his stash. I've got my own, thank you, so I don't need charity, I tell him.

"You know, you remind me of that movie, *Five Easy Pieces.*"

"Missed it. Is it about weed?"

"No. Jack Nicholson plays a guy who's seems to be running from his past, but without any apparent plan or direction. He's a pianist from a family of accomplished musicians, but when we meet him, he's working as an oil field worker in Texas or somewhere, and is screwing a waitress well below his station, Karen Black, and so—"

"Oh, *right*—I really see the resemblance to my situation. How does it end?"

"He runs away again. Leaves everything, including his winter coat. Tabula rasa. Into the wind."

"That doesn't solve anything," I purr in a reasonable Nicholson, arching my eyebrows. "Doesn't solve anything at all, Nurse Ratched."

Chris shrugs. "Well, duh. That's my point, bonehead."

Later when Kenny-Ken shows up—yes, I went ahead and found an O-Z of good red hair for him, costing forty-five clams, which is steep, but worth it—I ask him about the movie Chris mentioned, if my cinephile cousin has seen it.

He's thrilled: "Hell *yes*. Bob Rafaelson, 1970. Really put both him and Nicholson on the map, although he'd been around for a while at that point, having broken out after *Easy Rider* following a decade's worth of Roger Corman movies and other exploitation fare. Nicholson, I mean. A cool movie," he concludes in a pedantic rush. But a little frown crosses his brow, and his cheeks flush. "I've only seen parts of it," he admits. "*Easy Rider* is better."

"Chris said I reminded him of Jack Nicholson in that movie."

"*Easy Rider?*"

"The other one."

"Oh," he says, disappointed. But then: "Really? That's neat. Nicholson. He's working with Kubrick right now, shooting one of the Stephen King books—the vampire one, I think."

"He'll be perfect." The reefer is strong, real stony. Now I'm glad instead of guilty that, as an honorarium for services rendered, I pinched a good-sized bud out of Kenny-Ken's sack. "I'm gonna put on some music."

I peruse the LPs Chris has stacked by the turntable. Being a musician, my roommate is a record nut, always coming home with one of the bright yellow sacks from the used record store down in the Old Market, the commercial district near campus.

"Here we go—who the fuck is this Warren Zevon? Man alive, this record is great. Chris turned me onto it."

"Dunno. Let me see."

Kenny examines Zevon's youthful visage on the cover of the album, flips it over to see the musician dressed in a three-piece suit.

"Holy shit. There's a song called 'Werewolves of London'. What the fuck is that about? Werewolves? Horror movies?" The proximity of cinema causes Kenny-Ken to get all hot and bothered. "Put it on!"

I do as he asks, and upon second listening I'm digging these interesting tunes even more as they come pouring out of the speakers. We both agree that as cool pop songs go, these are real zingers. "Johnny Strikes Up the Band." "Excitable Boy." "Werewolves" is especially catchy. Being stoned makes music sound better than it might truly be, sometimes, but I think this is good stuff. There's one disco tune, but even this track isn't bad, not as vapid and repetitive as most of that dance crud.

"They'll be rocking in the projects… walking down along the strand…"

The strand. An interesting scheme comes to mind. A place to go. To hide, maybe.

To be someone else.

I debate discussing the situation with Kenny-Ken, about my plan to withdraw abruptly from the life I'm supposed to be living. Dangerous, this coming confession: Aunt Dorothy and my own mother spend hours chitchatting on the phone, even though they live only about a mile apart. I don't know what people have to say to each other for that long, especially folks who know one another as well as these sisters do. I can't stand talking on the damn phone. Nola-Marie broke up with me over the telephone, for Christ sakes.

But I plow ahead anyway, if for no other reason than to make it all the more real: I tell Kenny-Ken what's up, and the impressionable, stoned kid he is finds it all quite the romantic idea, if a little foolhardy.

"No plan, eh? Just, what–pull up stakes, take off, get a job somewhere? Doing—what?"

I tell him I don't know. "Work as a fry cook? Bartend? Odd jobs?"

"Wow. Real bohemian, dude."

"Don't make it all sound so well thought out, okay?"

"I I was to do it, ya know? Me, I mean?"

"Do tell."

"I would go straight to L.A. If I had a screenplay finished? No question, L.A. or New York. But then I'm comfortable with want I want to do, whereas you—"

"Yeah, like, I don't, I can't even—finish a sentence. And the thought of law school like my dad wants, it makes me sick."

"That's tough, man. Can't imagine." His eyes blaze. "Ever since *Jaws*, I've known I wanted to make movies. I've thought of nothing else for three years, bro."

"Well, lucky you."

Kenny-Ken splits, leaving me alone in the apartment. A neighbor's cat sits mewling outside on the front porch, and I go and slam the door with a loud boom.

I watch as the small gray tabby darts across the sidewalk and into the street. I hope that my action doesn't cause it to get killed. Cats are all right. They seem to know what they want most of the time. For them, food is the whole story, for the most part.

For what I hunger, however, I know not. Food ain't the problem, that's for sure, not for a middle class whiteboy like me—not in America, not in 1978. When I figure it out, I'll be sure to let everyone know.

2

———

ROLAND THE HEADLESS THOMPSON GUNNER

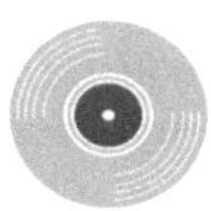

When he calls later that night (an unusual event in itself), my revered brother takes too long to arrive at a point.

"Nola told me how mean you were to her today on campus."

"So what?"

"So what is what."

"Try to be more specific," doing Woody Allen. "Try speaking in a series of grunts *and* clicks instead of just grunts."

"I'll kick your skinny little ass, Raymond. You hear me?"

Back to me: "Over what?"

"You need to be nicer to her."

"What for, exactly?"

"You just ought to."

Now I am both confused and suspicious. "What the hell is going on here?"

I hear him lighting a cigarette and exhaling a cloud of what I presume is nasty blue smoke, Vantage or some other crap brand. "I don't know how to say this. It seems weird, but I got to tell you, what's happened feels right. It just feels right. To us."

A cold gush of adrenaline in my gut. What fresh indignation is this? "Holy shit."

"That's right. Nola and me, we been going out."

I respond with a series of small mouth noises sounding like, "You. And Nola. Went out."

"Only once. Or well, a couple of times. I—I really like her."

Royally pissed: "Well, which is it? Once, or a couple?"

"A few."

"You assholes."

"Now, come on; you obviously don't care, being so nasty to her and all. She don't deserve that, Ray-Ray. No, she sure don't."

Jenkins and Nola-Marie. Well, if that don't beat all. What an insult. The hot realization washes over me like an electric blanket thrown over my head. "Did you fuck her yet? With that crooked little prick of yours?"

He denies it. I press him. He trots out the none-of-my-business line, which is bitter confirmation.

Kicked in the gut.

The conversation, full of rancor and harsh words, continues for a while. Finally, I say I have to get off the phone. That I don't care, and in reality I sort-of don't, actually.

"I want us all to be friends. There's no reason we c'ain't."

"No reason, eh?"

"We're family, don't forget that. We shouldn't let this get all up under us."

"We'll see about that."

Click.

So that seals it. I've got to do make a move. Now that my own brother has turned our lives into some Southern gothic hothouse family drama by porking my ex-girlfriend, I feel as though I'm going to come out of my own skin.

*

WALKING across campus towards the Old Market, the college ghetto full of bars and shops down the hill from University Terrace, I choose a meandering path through the neighborhood of old homes inhabited mostly by academic cognoscenti—the administrators, the tenured professors. The blocks reek of money, from the houses to the BMW and Mercedes automobiles gracing the driveways of the small estates like totems to success. Higher education—now there's a place to make some bread.

I stroll down the hill toward the pedestrian crossing at the railroad tracks, over which rumbles a slow-moving freight train. Columbia sits crisscrossed with surface railroad tracks; one day the city and state DOT must bite the bullet and relocate these obstacles to traffic flow. This town will be growing in the future. I read an article about people moving down here from the big, dirty rust belt cities in search of nice, cheap, clean little places like Columbia, in a sort of middle-class mirror of the black northern-going migration during Reconstruction, in the initial flowering of the industrial age.

I stand at the crossing in the dim twilight of a fading, early spring afternoon. The freight cars pass lugubrious and heavy, their surfaces pitted and scarred and dirty from being dragged a million miles back and forth across the expansive nation. Between the coming night, the low hanging clouds, and the neutral tones of the train cars, the entire world looms as a gray, misty transitory zone between two unknown realities. The only sound is the low *chunka-chunka-chunka* of the railcars rolling on by.

I feel lost, and alone.

But I'm not: A young Asian girl comes walking up and stands a few feet away. Her face is blank, an impassive mask of faraway thoughts, beautiful, straight black hair blowing in the slight breeze, which still holds a chill of the waning winter. Her face is lovely, exotic; I wonder if she is an international student.

A thousand adventures that she's lived race through my mind in an instant. Maybe she got out of Vietnam or Cambodia as one of those desperate boat people, barely ahead of the grim reaper. And now, even though she's alive and got a second chance—a new chance, in a new land teeming with plenty and opportunity—Columbia must seem awfully boring to her, not after such a life of danger and adventure. I simply must know more.

"Hi. I've seen you around"

I anticipate a shy, accented voice. Distracted, she glances in my direction. "Oh—hi."

"Where you from?"

She's startled out of her reverie by this direct question. "Rock Hill," she answers with an annoyed tilt of her head, in an accent flat and familiarly American. "Oh, right, you're in my Stats class. Or, wait—did you go to Calhoun High? In the class ahead of me?"

I'll be goddamn—exotic appearance or not, she's another more-or-less local like me. "No to both. I thought you were someone else. Sorry."

I turn back to the passing train without another word. I can sense her looking me over, probably frowning. Sorry—but another South Carolina girl? How dreadfully prosaic.

The train finally passes, and we are free to move forward. I give the girl a slight nod, and we go our separate ways, maybe forever.

A couple of weeks go by without incident. Nothing much changes, except I feel more trapped, more bored, more useless and uncertain about everything. Want me to describe my classes? I couldn't if I tried—I'm not even here in this body half the time anymore.

●

BUT ON THE cusp of spring break, a brief gust of freedom billows my sails:

Night envelopes the deserted South Carolina countryside. I hurtle my 1976 Ford Mustang, mustard yellow, at breakneck speed down the two-lane blacktop with all the windows down and the tunes rocking, even though the freezing air is turning my face numb. The shoulders of the road lay shrouded by the mists of midnight, the moisture hanging in the air supplied, presumably, by Lake Wateree a few miles to the east. After having told them I would arrive at my family's vacation house on the lake by early evening, I'm incredibly late. I am a bad son.

I had to take my time in packing, you see, because this trip might possibly last longer than a mere week.

I bet they'll be waiting up. Daddy, being a man of appetites, will have gone on to bed, but Mother will sit there. Waiting for my ass. Always so worried about everything.

I slow down a bit at that thought, and also because of the sharp curve coming up a quarter mile ahead, the scene of a car accident two years ago, the storied Kennington Boys Tragedy. Some kids doing ninety around the turn got killed here one night, the car flipping over and over until it came to rest entangled in a stand of trees about ten yards back from the road. The car had been full of beer cans and bits of gore, including a human tooth that had been knocked out. The rumor was that none of the kids in the car had lost a tooth, though, and they never figured out whose tooth it was, and maybe, just maybe, it was some kind of sign the devil had been involved.

When I first heard it, the tooth story really got under my skin. Gave me the creeps. Bullshit, I know, but spooky. I wonder if the gap-toothed, spectral owner is lurking out in the woods, watching me as I drive past, waiting for me to fuck up as well. I downshift and take the curve at thirty-five.

I weigh the options. If I was smart—and I'm not—I'd turn the car hard east and make my way out to the coast and mingle with the spring-breakers instead of spending it on the lake with the folks. I have plenty of clothes; on Friday, anticipating some sort of action on my part, I cashed in a couple of mature savings bonds my grandparents bought for me when I was little—so you know I was already thinking about doing this dastardly deed before I had even left Columbia.

Are you a man? Or a boy?

I stop at a closed gas station out in the middle of nowhere and go into the dusty, cobwebby phone booth. The only light comes from a flickering streetlamp above my head, the fluorescent tube in the phone booth long burned out and forgotten. I'm shocked to actually hear a dial tone.

The phone at the lake house rings and rings, until my father's voice, groggy—it's the way he sounds once he's had a few—is finally heard. We exchange niceties; he expresses concern at my whereabouts. I can hear my mother murmuring in the background.

I take a deep breath and tell them of my hastily-changed plans.

"Myrtle *Beach?* But son—what on earth for?"

I try to think of an explanation he'll buy. I depict a young girl of buxom and delightful proportions; I describe in moderate detail my scandalous intentions toward this idealized, imaginary sex object. I further articulate my own wishes to get past the Nola-Marie problems, and if Jenkins and she are going to be at the lake, well, I might find the act of joining them quite understandably uncomfortable.

He sits quiet for a moment, searching, I assume, for words that won't seem awkward. "Son, I know it must be difficult. And all."

"I think we're all better off. I'm sure they'll be quite happy together," I say with good cheer. Sounding like Melanie from GWTW: "Oh, don't you think so, Daddy?"

"I told Jenkins hormones be damned, but this was going to cause a durn rift in our family the likes of which could be detrimental to a team like ours, with such plans for high office."

"A family scandal. Already."

He said uh-huh. "But more than that, I don't want you to let this get under your skin, Raymond. I know it must hurt, though, son. I c'ain't imagine."

I try not to laugh. Already he's concerned the Nola-Marie rivalry between his sons will somehow disrupt his long-range political plans for the dynasty. Always scheming, thinking three steps ahead, that's my Dad. It all makes me want to just drift and dream and see where the wind sets me down.

"Don't sweat it, man. There's no hard feelings. Ask Jenkins—he'll tell you."

"Really?"

"I couldn't be happier for the two of them. I even told him so."

A dog barks off in the distance. I'm nervous all alone out in the countryside, remembering the scratchy 16mm print of *Texas Chainsaw Massacre* I'd watched at the student union only a few weeks ago. I'd never seen the horror movie before, and, high as hell, it scared the crap out of me. I need to get moving, and beg off from continuing the tiresome conversation with my old man by declaring my mind's made up, and that, as they say, is that.

Just at the moment of release, though, my mother gets on the phone, the one development I'd hoped to avoid.

"Ray-Ray, you get your skinny little ass out here to this god-durned lake house. What in god's name are you doing? Where are you?"

"Mama—?" Between the late hour and the perpetual dance between the two of us—patient reasoning versus stubborn irrationality, in a titanic battle for control of the intellectual high ground—I sigh and listen to her go on. I'm tempted to tell her the truth, that I'm thinking about not coming back from Myrtle Beach at all—that I'm dropping out of Southeastern, I'm searching and seeking and trying to define myself, and this is some small step toward that end, a hundred-fifty mile, epic journey of discovery that will, in all probability, be a waste of time and money. But it will be different from the do-nothing life I've been living, which feels too much like the track of someone else's life.

A snatch of a song lyric flits through my mind—*she picks up a book of her father's life and throws it on the fire*—and finally I manage to ring off by telling my mother I'll call her each and every day from the beach. "Promise."

She buys it. I breathe a sigh of release.

As I emerge from the phone booth, however, a county patrolman rolls into the dark and very-much-closed gas station, positioning his prowler in front of the Mustang. He hits me in the face with his spotlight. Great.

I give a friendly wave.

"Boy, you got car trouble?" I can barely make out the cop through the glare of the light—he looks like a small mound of redneck flesh poured in behind the wheel of his cruiser. I can smell cigar smoke from the interior of the car.

"No, sir," I answer in a clear and steady voice. I'm not too scared, and in spite of the weed I have stashed in the bottom of my old Army knapsack inside some rolled up socks. In fact, right now I'm sober as a judge. I gesture down the highway toward the east. "I realized I forgot to check in with my parents."

He swings his light over at the Mustang, the pay phone, then back at me. "Them eyes look mighty red, son. What else you been doing?"

"Nothing, other than studying all afternoon back in Columbia, sir. At Southeastern. Trying to get some homework done before spring break kicks in."

"Spring break?"

"I'm on my way to meet some friends in Myrtle Beach."

Skeptical, he turns off the hellish spotlight, and in stifling a yawn I can discern his interest in this well-spoken college youth waning—after all, compared to many of today's kids, my sideburns and shaggy hair could be considered clean-cut.

"All right now, son. Be careful out on these roads at night like this."

"Are there boogeymen about, officer?"

"Always, boy. Keep it between them lines and you'll be all right."

Looking, I presume, for any signs of inebriation or suspicious body language, he sits and watches as I walk, steady, back to my car. I pull out onto the road, my heart thump-thumping in my chest, and give him a farewell salute.

With my speed hovering at fifty-five, he follows me for a half-mile or so until turning in the opposite direction, finally, at the junction with Highway 34. I sigh with relief as a solitary, yellow caution light, flashing forlorn in the inky country dark of the South Carolina nighttime, recedes in the rearview.

·

By CONTRAST, the light coming up on the Atlantic Ocean is comforting and lovely from my vantage point on the 14th Avenue pier in the heart of downtown Myrtle Beach, where I sit alone to ponder my decision for coming here. The wind from the water gusts downright chilly. The reflection of the sodium street lamps on the surface of the vast, dark sea reminds me of *Starry Night*, somehow.

I pulled into town about two-thirty, with the revelry up and down Ocean Boulevard in full swing: packs of teenagers wandered and caroused, girls scoping out guys, the same in reverse, with stereos thumping as the muscle cars cruised and revved engines under the not so watchful eyes of bored MBPD cops sitting in a gravel parking lot between the water slide and the putt-putt. First impression? I felt sad and nostalgic for my own, fabled Sun Fun week—getting smashed, screwing Nola-Marie repeatedly on a cheap motel mattress, and having nary a care in the world. Two years ago. How quickly it all changed.

I found a place to park the Mustang on a side street and mingled into the dwindling crowd. Famished, I grabbed a hot dog from Peaches Corner across from the Myrtle Beach Pavilion, which, given the late hour, sat closed and dark.

I smiled at a girl in a booth in the diner. Looking about fourteen, she gave me an interested eye. I didn't think I needed to get into all that, not just yet, and especially with one ostensibly so young. Horny, maybe, but not desperate.

Afterwards, I walked the boardwalk, lonesome, my fingers smelling of yellow mustard. Finally I said, fuck it, I'm on vacation, and bought a sixer of PBR at an all-night convenience store in the back half of one of the family-run motels dotting the shoreline and the downtown commercial district.

The proprietor, a disgusted man in his sixties, a real bulldog with a crew cut and horn rims, looked for all the world as though he hated my guts the second I walked into the place. I wanted to ask him, well, how are you supposed to get paid if turkeys like me don't come in and pick up sixers, but instead I only smiled and said, "Nice night."

He grunted out the price—one ninety-eight plus tax, very dear, oh yes, this highway robbery—and left our interaction at that. He didn't ask for my ID even though people usually tell me I look younger than I am. That's probably why the girl seemed so interested—she thought I a little high school boy, a peer.

As high tide approaches, waves crash against the pilings with force. Furtive, I drink by keeping the can concealed in a brown paper sack. I think about twisting up a number, but I'm not sure how wise it is, even in the wee hours like this.

At first I don't notice the old timer who has shuffled up behind me, and I'm startled as he plops down on a bench next to the one on which I'm sprawled.

"Shit'll give you splinters."

"How's that?"

"Sitting out here, man."

As I give him the once-over, I begin to understand that in spite of his shuffling gait and a missing tooth or three, he isn't an old timer at all—around the eyes and mouth the guy looks about thirty, but his slight body is stooped and weary. His hair is blonde, I think, whereas before I thought it was gray. He's got a filthy Army field jacket on over some colorful Guatemalan drawstring pants; I wonder if his dirty feet aren't cold, since all he's got on are a pair of the cheapest flip-flops you can imagine.

"Didn't have anywhere else to go," I offer, meek and uncertain of this odd fellow's attention.

"Join the club. We ain't supposed to be out here now, matter of fact."

It's true; I'd squeezed in through a tear in the chain-link fence with the PIER CLOSED sign hanging on it, and I suspected he'd done the same. At the time, I was feeling naughty—I wanted to go somewhere they said I shouldn't.

"Want a cool one?" I produce a can from my dwindling stash. I only need a couple to feel good anyway.

"You know it, feller. Hot damn if I don't."

I think about what life must be like for this guy, out on his ass. I'm a little college fuck from Columbia, and I have a life and a warm bed to which I can return at first light, if I get too scared or bored. I think about life on the street, and the rules and challenges and codes of conduct that must be followed. To be an outlaw, you must be honest, as Bob Dylan said.

We sit and drink our beers until he starts up asking me questions, and I respond in kind with my own queries. I discover he's a Vietnam veteran, disabled but refused treatment by what he called "a bastard of a gub'mint that eats up men like me and spits 'em back out halfway, leaving them just alive enough to suffer. Son of a bitches—every one of 'em." Even though he's only had a half a beer, he already sounds hammered. When the wind shifts and I catch a whiff of the stink coming off him, I realize he's already plowed.

"My grandfather was in the service," I tell him. "Landed on D-Day, fought all the way into Germany. After he'd had a few snorts and the women-folk were out of the room, he'd tell me stories. Fucked up shit, man."

I relate anecdotes regarding the supposed stealing of Patton's jeep one night, the carousing, the promotions, busts, promotions, and busts back down in rank that seemed to characterize my apparent ne'er-do-well of a grandfather's military service.

"He tell you about all the bad shit you see? When you're in combat?"

"A few things. Talked about seeing a German get his head blown off, when they were in the hedgerows right after Normandy. Said he saw the guy pop up over the hedgerow, and that he and his buddies all drew a bead at the same time. Took it clean off."

The vet grunts and shakes his head and drinks his beer.

"Thing was, my granddad said 'you understand how happy we were to get him before he got any of us, right? That's the way it was out there'."

"Yeah, got that right."

"But years later, he told me, he would think about that guy, just out of the blue. Not dream about it or anything, but suddenly he'd get a flash of that dude's head being there one minute, but gone the next. Poof. How the German was a real person, and all. He said he wondered what the guy's life was before he got drafted into the army. If he had a family. What the guy's name was. That kinda stuff."

"It don't matter, beau. Once you're dead, it don't matter what your goddurn name was."

"Guess not. Unless you've done something amazing along the way."

The homeless vet, agitated, gets up and ambles off into the night. "That war? Them boys like your granddaddy? They was fightin' for something. I don't know *what* we was fighting for in that jungle."

Unsteady, he pitches his can over the side of the pier and trudges away, and I'm left alone to ponder the words he has spoken, and the ideas behind them. I'm too young to have protested the Vietnam war; it ended a few years ago, when I was still a child. Seemed like they said it was over, but we didn't get our butts out of there for quite awhile afterwards.

I don't know—all that world political stuff, I don't pay much attention to it. Don't know what the big deal is. Not much interested in politics. That, as I have established, is Daddy's world.

❋

THE DAWN COMES pink and soft, the sun emerging from a thin wisp of cloud cover along the horizon. I sit in quiet contemplation of the daybreak on a bench along boardwalk—really a street-level concrete sidewalk above the dunes—and watch as old people shuffle back and forth looking for shells. One man, corpulent and bald, sweeps a metal detector back and forth, occasionally stooping over to dig and examine a find that is, I presume, of infinite interest to him.

The waves, incredibly gentle, struggle to lap onto the gray sand as the outgoing tide pulls at the water, coaxing tiny whitecaps back toward the mother ocean rather than this shoreline that is the domain of man. Only now do I think about the fact that I haven't slept or eaten for many hours now, and I find my way up the boulevard to a breakfast joint.

Breakfast is filling at the Olympic Flame Pancake House a few blocks north, just like I remembered it from Sun Fun, except the grits need salt like crazy to taste right. So much sea-salt in the drinking water around here you wouldn't think so, but there you go.

Quiet in here, since it's so early; lot of kids will stay passed out after their late night of revelry to which I only feel the slightest of connections. If I wanted to party, I could have stayed in Columbia, right? My journey to the shore is of a different kind than some short-lived hedonistic getaway from reality—by contrast, reality is exactly that which I seek. Not some movie fantasy—*Star Wars* is still playing, and almost a year later, can you believe that?—but a glimpse of life apart from the one I've known and been groomed to cultivate into some vastly more powerful version of my father, or the way he sees himself. I can't live with my future planned out for me, not by him. Besides, he has Jenkins.

And now I have the beach.

●

SINCE I STILL DON'T KNOW WHERE to go or what to do, I flip through yesterday's *Columbia Record* and sip refills of weak coffee. Finally I give in to the waitress's impatient eyes and allow her table to turn over. I leave a generous, two-dollar tip for the indulgence of my protracted presence in her section.

About ten o'clock the strand starts to wake up in earnest, and the barely-warm-enough sand fills with the flesh of the young, their bodies alternately pink or pale. (Blacks keep to themselves up at Atlantic Beach, mostly—we must not forget South Carolina is only a decade into the era of integration, and like many similar places, racial divides still exist. Tillman Falls is a prime example of this, but you probably already guessed that.) Girls who tonight will parade in peasant blouses and platform shoes and hip-hugger bellbottoms are, for the moment, clad in only swimsuits and otherwise casual wear. Many of these sunbathers hail from northern climes, so the air, already warmed to the mid-sixties, must seem balmy and delightful.

The sun shimmers off the water with a million-billion sapphire high-lights; still windy, the whitecaps are as short-lived dollops of cream, vanishing almost as soon as they appear. I stroll at the high-tide line through a vast band of broken seashells like the swath of the Milky Way galaxy I could discern overhead on a moonless night up in the mountains, once. I tread with care in my Chucks, navigating around the occasional clump of seaweed or dead jellyfish. Surfers attempt in vain to ride the gentle swells; I wonder how they can stand being in the water as cool as the air still feels this time of year.

A hint of pot drifts past my nose, and for a brief moment some sweet incense wafts like a bottle of vanilla extract dumped into the air. My stomach gurgles; now that I've eaten such a hearty breakfast, I realize how tired I am.

I have to find someplace to sleep.

And a job.

That's right. I need a job. I need a room—cheap, long term—and work, some shit job to make ends meet throughout the season. Yes: I will stay here at the beach. I will call first thing next Monday and withdraw from all my classes; I can decide by, say, the first of August whether or not I want to go back to school in the fall, stay here, or move on when the spirit calls.

Or at least, that's what I'll tell my folks when I call them to explain I've become a college dropout and an active beach bum. I'll dangle the carrot of a possible autumn return to my studies upon the hill at august Southeastern U, as well as the fact that I only ran away to Myrtle Beach and not California, "like I'd originally planned." That will scare the mud out of them.

I run through the scenario in my mind as I stroll back, check on the car —when I inquire, a beat cop tells me that it's fine where it is, which is parked on a side street—and cruise back across Ocean Boulevard, which is relatively free of traffic so early in the day. Tonight, though, will be a different story, as the tide of GTOs and Camaros creep up and down the strip, looking for whatever it is people driving the same mile of road are seeking—romance, a challenge, a momentary thrill.

Back on the beach I cross paths with a lifeguard, a guy about my age, already buff and brown even though it's only March. I inquire of him about rooms around the neighborhood, or wherever, and Duffy, as he claims his name to be, gives me a few suggestions. He lives with his folks, he says with a slightly downcast, embarrassed eye, "but it's at the Club, so it's nice, you know. Lot of great looking girls."

"Like everywhere," I smile as two bleach-blonde ladies saunter by, their skinny teenaged bodies paler than pale—it's only the second day of spring break, after all. I can hear from their accents they are from, say, Pennsylvania or Jersey or thereabouts, and they giggle and whisper as Duffy flashes a toothy grin that downright sparkles in the sunlight. I note how the girls are giving Duffy the eye, and not ordinary old yours-truly.

"Ladies," he says in salutation as they pass at a languid pace. Next he whispers in conspiratorial dismissal, "Strictly second-string action there, though. Sorry, folks," he concludes with a Fonzi-style thumbs down.

I think they're fine and dandy—they're from somewhere else besides South Carolina, after all!—but for the sake of masculine camaraderie, I go along with his assessment. "Yeah, not so hot."

"Plenty more where that came from."

"Yeah. I've got all summer to worry about it," I offer casually.

"Not in any hurry, eh?"

"Coming off a bummer with this chick back home. Part of the reason I'm here, I reckon."

"'On the rebound'—that's a poontang magnet right there, trust me. Pick one, get all moist-eyed and talk about your broken heart. Works every freaking time."

"I hear you. Got to get settled in first, though. Get a crash pad to bring 'em back to. Any suggestions?"

"*Hmm*. If you want to be on the water, walk on down past the next pier. After a few blocks there's some older family hotels and stuff, like, long-term rates in some of them, I bet. Not pretty, but cheaper than these joints here in the middle of everything. Short of that, you'll need to look closer to the highway. Few blocks back off the front row ain't so bad. Five minute walk."

"Got it, bro. Thanks." I give him a right-on fist and we go our separate ways. At least in the short term I think I want to be on the beach, where the action seems to be. Not like I'm putting down roots. I pledge to be like dandelion fluff—who knows where the wind may blow me.

For reasons unknown, the proprietor of the El Mar Inn seems suspicious of me, and quotes an exorbitant rate considering the condition of the accommodations in question: sand-weathered, peeling-paint, salt-damaged little rooms smelling of foot odor and other bodily excretions. The old guy doesn't care for me, not one bit. I demur and move on, which seems to annoy him even more.

Pirate's Cove Motel is cheap but even more dingy, and appears run by Middle Eastern mafia types, a scenario my imagination, hungry for intrigue, strives to create. As I saunter through the office doorway, the two swarthy dudes behind the counter halt their conversation and stare; I beg off without even asking the rate.

The Sea Gypsy. The Sea Nymph. The Sea Palms. The Sea Cove. The Coral Sands. The Pierview. The Wayfarer. The last seems the most appropriate, at least in name. Still nothing feels right.

Before a big bend in the road and the high-rise Holiday Inn, I come across the Grand Strand Family Motel, a grandiloquent and evocative name for what is in reality a broken-down, beat-up dump with sea oats poking up through a broken concrete sidewalk, and a gravel parking lot containing exactly one car, a VW pop-top microbus with Jersey plates. The color of the paint on the stucco outside of the motel was once blue with white trim; now the two are more as shades of gray, the blue faded by the sun and the white mottled and dark with grime. Seems like a quaint, quiet place. Should be cheap. I go inside.

After not so protracted negotiations with the proprietor, a bored and sleepy-looking woman who tells me her name is Sheila, I am shown what will be my home, at least for the short term, a clean but shabby room with a kitchenette. Perfect. If I can get the right job, I can move to an affordable long-term apartment a little farther off the beach.

On the other hand, being right here next to the roiling surf makes this adventure seem like a holiday alongside the real goal: the grandly-conceived, existential, angst-ridden examination of a life which thus far, in my bitter and dissatisfied opinion, remains quite unexamined. If I can get some swimming and a little sun in along with the philosophical rumination, all the better.

Sheila sucks on a menthol cigarette and leans in the doorway of the small room while I examine it, and her mouth, like my mother's, is already getting that puckered smoker's look, with wrinkles beyond her years. Still, she's attractive in a beaten-down way.

"So what are you doing, Mr. long-term Ray DeKalb," she asks with an interesting glint in her eye. "Taking a extra spring break week or two?"

I answer in my patented, practiced English upper class twit accent, one learned from *Monty Python* reruns on PBS, a voice oozing with amusement and charm. "I find, good lady, that I'm on the run from romantic entanglements, as well as a perfectly ghastly and boring career away at university. Looking to settle down a bit, collect my wits, have a jolly time doing so. Yes yes, pip pip, and all that."

Her smile at my silly voice blooms like a fresh-cut flower. "Sounds perfectly charming."

I slide into my normal mid-Carolina twang, a voice I'd just as soon conceal. "Really planning to relax, enjoy the scenery for a while. I need time to figure out a few things."

"Well, have a nice stay with us. Let me know if you need anything, Mr. DeKalb."

If I didn't know better, I'd swear this woman was flirting with me. "I'm looking for work, too. Don't suppose you need a handy man around here." As if I have handy-man skills. Never took shop, you know.

She laughs through a lungful of smoke, a sad little *huh-huh-huh*. "Not much to be done anymore around this old place anyhow. Not much point."

"You the owner, ma'am?"

Nodding. "My husband—well, my ex-husband, and me, we inherited it from my Daddy. There's only me now, though, and my cousin Boosey who works at night, and the maid. LaTisha's been working here for Daddy since I don't know when."

"A legacy business here on the strip."

"You could call it that."

"That's what it is."

Sheila's weary, her façade weathered like the exterior of her motel. "I shouldn't tell you this, but—we probably won't last the season."

"Oh, no. Really?"

"Truth is, there's a developer might want to buy me out, if they can get three or four of these places all in a row to sell. They wanna build a big condo building, like the Yachtsman and all that further"—it sounds like *fuhtha*—"on up yonder."

"Probably get a decent price, huh?" Sheila's old and all, but damn if she isn't attractive despite the years I see measured in the lines around her eyes. It doesn't help that I'm horny as a three-balled tomcat. And something in the way those gray eyes twinkle is making me tingle.

"I hope so. Hard though. I grew up around here. Hate to see it go away, because of my daddy and all."

"Well, he won't know. It'll be okay."

"You think so?" She folds her arms across what I notice is a rather matronly and full bosom, one that looks soft and inviting. I flash on resting my weary head there, perhaps even in the afterglow of some intimate congress between the two of us.

Who am I kidding, though? What am I, back in seventh grade again, thinking about Mrs. Fremont while my mom beats on the bathroom door asking why I'm taking so long in there every night? Schoolboy fantasies will get me nowhere.

I pull myself together. "I'm sure whatever makes you the happiest is the best way to honor his memory."

"You'll understand once you get a little older, Raymond. Once your own folks start to—leave you behind."

"Yeah. My folks are definitely still around. They loom large in my life, make no mistake."

"They always will."

I have to stop myself from blurting, *God, I hope not.*

She waves it all away, offers me her hand in a quick, businesslike hand-shake. "Just let me know how long you think you'll be with us. I'll let you have the room facing the beach until the season gets cranked up, if you're here long enough. We're not as busy right now as I'd hoped."

"You will be, again."

"I doubt it. Time is short."

My gratitude comes profuse—ocean front, after all—after which I go to collect my trusty vehicle, and with it my meager belongings.

Lunchtime on day one, and already I have a home. Next, to seek gainful employment. No time like the present; the early bird gets the worm. If employment comes as easily as my new beachfront bachelor pad, I'll know I'm on the right track.

And Sheila Wilson is easy on the eyes, a good-looking woman, I decide, who is sexy as all get-out. *I wonder how old she really is?*

3

EXCITABLE BOY

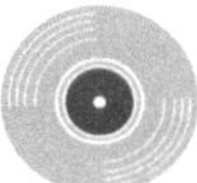

The manager of the Myrtle Beach Pavilion, Mr. Pugliesi, looks me in the eye as I offer a strong handshake and try to seem eager, poised and nonchalant, but on the inside I'm intimidated as can be. This man is seasoned and tough and don't take no guff, as he explains in melodious yet guttural utterances. He's short and stocky and solid; his gut pokes out, but it isn't flabby, not by a long shot. You could bounce a quarter off his sparkling white T-shirt. His hands are thick and coarse, a workingman. He could break me in half.

Italian by birth, Pugliesi seems in his years here in the Carolinas to have lost little of his ethnicity or accent. In the first five minutes of our interview, quite apart from having any relevance whatsoever to the question at hand—of my employment—he gives me an encapsulated history of his people's immigration, first to the shores of America, their subsequent familial history of circus and carny work, and then after a generation or two, the migration further south. With his hair greased and quite obviously dyed shoe-polish black—I guess from the deep lines in his rough face that he's in his late fifties—he gestures and curses in Italian and chews the stub of an unlit cigar. I'm digging it—he is the sort of authentic, worldly character with whom I'm looking to interact in my time here.

I figured getting work at the amusement park would put me at ground zero of the ebb and flow of human interaction in this neighborhood, and I tell him so. I am not only hungry for work, but also experience among what I term "real people."

"First thing about this place," he tells me, "it ain't like-a the real world, but the people, they're real, all right. But, what? I don't know what to do with a college boy like you. Now—why is it you ain't in school no more, again?"

I explain the situation—the yearning, the hopes, the dreams—and I do so quite consciously in my own voice, and not in the comedic accent like I used earlier with Sheila. As we walk around the several-acre site of the pavilion while discussing my situation, the gaming booths and rides come to life. The smell of corn dogs makes my stomach rumble. A smattering of spring breakers enjoy the attractions, but not too many, not yet.

Mr. Pugliesi barks orders and instructions and admonishments at a variety of park personnel. Proud, he shows off the Hershell-Spillman Carousel in its new building right on the Boulevard, a project completed only a week ago. The old carousel, intricate and lovely in design, will now be better protected from the harsh elements—the salt, the sand, the wind, the rain.

"So what's to prevent you from deciding yer tired of working for me all-a sudden, like you got bored with your fancy-pants college over in Columbia?"

"Sir, I assure you I will stand by a commitment for employment throughout the season. I don't plan, barring unforeseen circumstances, to leave the beach before Labor Day, at least." I work my eyebrows up and down, letting him know how savvy I am about the benchmark dates for the tourist season. "I'm living down the way, at the Grand Strand."

"Close by. At a motel?"

"Until I get established in a more permanent apartment. Either way, I won't be so much as a second late."

"Well—I ain't got nothing right now, not for no college boy. This here's real work. Hard work."

He nods at a young man with suspicious eyes and two gold hoops through his earlobes like a pirate—the Tilt-A-Whirl operator. The guy in turn eyes us both with skepticism, my polo shirt and deck shoes making me look, I realize, like a country club college frat boy compared to most of the other people working the Pavilion. Every one of them has a hard-faced, blue-collar look you see among folks who work the circus and the state fairs and have, in my imagination, seen and done it all out traveling the highways and byways.

Pugliesi concludes: "No job somebody like you'd want, anyways."

"How do you know?"

"Besides, after next week we only open on weekends till Memorial Day."

"Perfect. I don't need much work. Weekends would be fine."

Actually it isn't perfect, but I don't want to queer this deal. I can scrape by on whatever I get, I've decided. I must peel away the layers of my privileged life in order to find the answer inside me, as Chris so eloquently put it. No better way to peer into the soul than through privation, and even hunger, by working among these honest-to-god real people.

"But seriously—I'm open to anything. Anything you've got, I can do." What a blatant lie. I hope my cheeks aren't as red as they feel.

"Let's us see how serious you are about-a working in my park." He strokes his thin, black mustache, still regarding me with some degree of uncertainty, as though he's wary of being pranked or otherwise having his time wasted. "Let's get-a you in with old George over here. If he likes you, well, we'll put you on the cleaning crew, starting tomorrow."

"Cleaning crew?"

"You said anything. Didn't you?"

"That I did."

So maybe not anything glamorous, but just like that—a job. I can't lose at this game.

BACK AT THE STRAND, I turn over in my mind the circumstances of my new charge in life, which is to push a broom around after fat tourists, who go about dropping their holiday detritus behind them as though placing landmarks through the dark woods to provide a marked pathway back home. Much worse chores will be in the offing as well—I'm betting the restrooms get mighty dirty on a busy evening in high summer.

The men, Mr. Pugliesi and the janitorial supervisor George, an enormous black man with horn-rim glasses and a raspy, smoke-ravaged voice choked with phlegm, laughed and held their noses as they mentioned that salient fact. Pugliesi winked and told me to report to George tomorrow, fifteen minutes before the park opens for business. "Not a second later."

"Wear some long pants, too, boy." George, clearing his throat twice. "You ain't on vacation like our guests. Jeans and a plain T-shirt for now, till Mr. P gets you a uniform. And I mean a plain T-shirt, now, god-dog it. Don't want none of them rock bands or nothing else on there, you hear me?"

Well, so much for the black Led Zeppelin '77 tour shirt I'd coveted in one of the head shops on the other side of Ripley's Believe It or Not. "Yes sir, Mr. George. I'll see you tomorrow, ready to work." I gave him a little salute, which he returned with a scowl and a wave.

A janitor. I have gone from being the next governor of our fair state to a custodial worker. Could there be a wider gulf in ambition?

That will show my dad, I try to convince myself.

The beach is now alive with youthful revelers, much more crowded than before, even this far down. There are larger hotels two blocks farther back from the beach up and down Ocean Boulevard; many of my cost-conscious spring break brethren have chosen to stay off the sand, so to speak, in order to save money. Beer isn't free, after all, and neither is weed, not at thirty or forty dollars an ounce. Ah—another issue, hooking up with a decent herb connection. All good things in all good time.

●

THE FIRST WEEK goes by in a state of relative lassitude, and after I go ahead and tell my parents of my real plans, I endure a series of screaming, telephone shouting matches with every member of my immediate family.

The next weekend turns eventful: I discover the joys of discarded, disposal infant diapers filled with ill-digested chili-dog components—who feeds their baby a Myrtle Beach Pavilion hot dog?—I run out of pot, meet a few people but no one I'm willing to hit up for more, and then after an interminable second week, the next Friday I collect a partial-week paycheck even smaller than I thought it might be.

Also, I remain without meaningful female companionship—except for

Sheila, with whom I have developed a flirtatious, daily session of witty repartee. She thinks I'm "so cute" with all of my imitations and voices.

Truth: I am dying to nail this woman, twice my age; I am almost starting to believe that it's possible. She seems wounded, fragile. Only yesterday she rested her hand on my forearm, and my dick flooded with hot blood, as did my cheeks.

I sweet-talk her into cashing my meager paycheck right as she's leaving to go out for the night, "on another ridiculous date with my ex-husband," she offers, even though I have not inquired about her plans for the evening. "Carl thinks—well, it don't matter what he thinks. Only what I think."

After she leaves, I shoot the shit with cousin Boosey for a while. He's interested that I've ditched Southeastern in the middle of the semester, having gone there himself "as a history major," he tells me, "before they kicked me out back during the riots." After Kent State, he goes on to say, the anti-war movement made its way even to the hinterland of South Carolina, he explains. I'd heard tell of all this from one of my professors, and even at the modest remove of only eight years, such activities as street marches and rock-throwing feel to my generation like events from another age.

Boosey shifts gears and tells me he's writing a science-fiction novel. He expends half an hour describing the expository nature of the first fifty pages, in excruciating and difficult-to-follow detail that puts me in a near somnambulant state of boredom. "And then they finally lift off on the mission—that's as far as I got so far."

Super. All that and his characters haven't even blasted off yet. A great work this will surely be, I tell him. He's certain it will be a hit, since George Lucas will have made sci-fi bigger than ever. Maybe old Boosey is right to pursue the genre. If only I were a writer, I'd give it a try myself.

Finally I extricate myself, providing as a rationale the fatigue from which I suffer at the end of this long workday. I'm already wistful for my relatively quiet and easy day shifts; Mr. George, now satisfied with my skills and level of motivation, has told me next week I go to the night shift, which is from four in the afternoon until a couple of hours after the park closes, when I and the other custodians will do what he terms "the big clean-up."

Joy. I hope I can get by on my paltry wages, coupled, of course, with my trust fund payout that Chris will forward to me in a day or two. I wonder. I admit to myself I won't be able to stay at the Grand Strand much longer, or on the ocean front at all, for that matter.

◦

As THE DAYS grow longer and the temperatures warmer, Sheila's motel fills up; she has told me that the rolling spring-break weeks until Easter should give her a decent stake to make it through until things start hopping again at the end of May. She got an odd look on her face, and became all dewy-eyed and obviously thinking about the impending sale, then seemed to shake it off.

I interact one morning with a young couple also staying in the motel. After I emerge from my room showered and prepared to go scope out consumables including a fresh stash of grass, I observe the two strangers having a full-out, gritted-teeth, screaming-yet-hushed argument on the beach not far from the open door of my room, amidst the sea oats in the soft dunes a dozen yards past the tide line. I try to listen to what they're saying as I peer out from behind the threadbare blue curtain across my front window.

The girl yells, "Not after the way you talked to me earlier." The guys' voice comes low and menacing, but that's all I get out of him, his tone and inflection one of anger.

The guy gestures and snarls with a hard glint in his eye. "I said I was sorry," she concludes in tears. I hear him say, "Your 'sorry' ass can *stay* here in this dump, Jamie."

The guy's a real tough customer in spite of his ostensible guise as a love-beaded and sandal-shod, shaggy-haired peacenik type; his eyes glimmer cold and hard, and he has a prominent, ugly scar along on one side of his jaw line. His hair is ice-blonde, and the complexion of his face ruddy. Looks as though he had some rough bouts with acne in the not too distant past. A heavy brow.

This so-called Jamie's as cute as can be, though, near as I can tell from my vantage point. Skinny, barefoot, and petite, wearing a home-made tie-dye t-shirt and bellbottoms, I think to myself that she deserves a nice boyfriend, nicer than this ape, even though I don't know her from Eve.

After some final words and a grasp at her upper arm, she stalks away toward the ocean and he comes back to the motel.

I stand stretching and fake-yawning outside my room. Since the guy looks the way he does, I think about trying to ask him about grass, except he looks so angry I find myself hesitant.

"Hey, brother. What's shaking?"

He passes by kicking sand in front of him, a frustrated shuffle over his woman problems.

So much for the pot idea.

I watch from afar as the girl strides back and forth in the surf, occasionally stooping down to examine a find in the water. After a minute or two I hear the rumble of an engine reluctantly cranking into life—it turns out these cats they are the owners of the VW microbus I noticed earlier in the week—and it pulls out and fades away. It's the moment the guy who Jamie will tell me is named Lars has left her behind here in Myrtle Beach, with only a few bucks to her name, but one new friend: me.

◦

JAMIE LEIGH ALLENDALE—HER first name is really Janet, she says, like the *Psycho* actress, but they started calling her Jamie for some inscrutable reason—seems at ease with me; after the description of the scene with said Lars Dammick, I must seem a sophisticated and non-threatening individual.

As it turns out, my intuition was correct, and Lars would indeed have been the right guy to meet: She said they came down from New Jersey for a couple of weeks so he could deal under-weight nickel and dime bags to spring breakers, turning a tidy profit on this big headstash of dope he'd scored on the cheap. Things had gone well until she forgot to lock the van, and someone rifled the headstash and ripped it off. She tells me all this, I think, because I have intimated wistful memories of the red-hair goodies of which I have run out.

"Took it all. What was left."

"That's tough. How much did y'all lose?"

"Couple lids. I mean it wasn't so bad—Lars started out with a half-pound. We been here almost two weeks already. He's a little shit," she adds quickly. "He had it coming."

Jamie's no beauty queen, not the way we judge women around these parts at least, but with her mousy face *sans* makeup and flip-up bangs and her golden-brown skin, I can't help but suffer salacious thoughts. In my constant state of near-concupiscence, Jamie is starting to look like the prettiest girl I've ever seen.

"What if I told you a secret."

I shrug. I wouldn't tell a stranger any of my secrets. "Sure."

"Nobody took the pot."

"*What?*"

She goes over and pulls a battered salmon-colored Samsonite suitcase from under the bed. The case has daisy stickers of various size applied to it, but half are peeling up or otherwise faded and torn from handling and poor adhesive contact with the rough molded plastic.

"Look." She produces what looks like about two ounces of decent bud, half of which is already rolled up in smaller nickel and dime bags, little Zip-locks in which you get extra buttons whenever you buy a suit-coat or dress shirt.

"Holy shit." I'm now petrified Lars, a big dude, will stroll in and see that I am a party to this malfeasance on Jamie's part. "Why'd you tell him it got stolen?"

"Because I saw him with this little slut over by the Bowery, when he thought I was back here at the motel. He was supposed to be working—I guess he was, sort of—but it looked like he was doing a lot more than slinging pot. And I wanted to teach him a lesson." Her Jersey-girl voice comes tough and coarse; already in my mind I am working on my own version of her accent.

"So—where was he going?"

"Back home, that's what he said." She sneezes and scratches at her upturned nose.

"He *left* you?"

She finally looks upset about the whole deal, depressed and uncertain. "Looks that way."

"Well—that wasn't cool."

She explains that Lars tends to do what he says.

Then, she cries, brief and quiet. Wiping away tears, my new friend produces an embarrassed smile. "I screwed up real good this time. I didn't mean to. I just do, sometimes."

My mind reels at the notion of this young girl having been dumped so far from home, and, tears aside, not all that concerned about it. Me? I'd be scared shitless. "What are you gonna do?"

"I was getting tired of Lars and his macho bullshit anyway. I really just wanted to get away from Newark for a while. And so I did."

Now that the fact of our shared goals of escape and adventure has become clear, I take the opportunity to outline for her my situation, hoping that she will note the similarities and be intrigued by me. I take liberties; I embellish the acrimonious nature of my relationship with my father, and downplay my station in life.

I'm delighted to find she supports my decision. She says, "Just had to get out from under it all too. My folks—well my mom—she ain't got a pot to piss in, so why stick around, ya know?"

"Same with my folks." A lie; a pang of mild guilt at my duplicity. "But listen, whatever you need, since we're both sort of cast adrift here, let me know what I can do."

She gives me a sweet smile. "Right now I need somebody to smoke down with."

Jamie and me. Two refugees from the world, here at land's end. The pot is kind of shitty, though, not as good as it looked—but better than nothing at all.

◦

I ENCOUNTER Sheila after Jamie and I make our brief and quite platonic farewells for the evening, which, seeing as how Lars may or may not have actually split the scene, I don't mind in spite of my budding attraction to her—you know how these things go, these little spats. Last thing I need is an ass-kicking by some pissed off Jersey boy who shows back up.

The motel proprietor has returned from another 'date' with her ex, and seems tipsy as she makes her way toward the family residence behind the motel office. She drops her keys, followed by her purse.

"Oh, fiddlesticks," she says as I come up behind her. "Shoot."

"Sheila, looks like you fumbled a pass."

"Well, hey there, sugar."

I discover her face streaked with mascara: she's been crying.

"You okay?" She's an adult, and I feel odd about calling her by a given name and not a more formal title. "How are—I mean, how's tricks?"

"Tricks? Like on Halloween?"

"Halloween's a long way off. No tricks."

Wiping her eyes. "How about treats?"

"I wouldn't turn one down."

"Listen: I need a cup of coffee. You want one? Or do you drink tea?"

●

SHEILA TELLS me in excruciating detail for over an hour about the woes surrounding her love life. I am all nods and *uh-huhs* in my attempt to be as sympathetic as possible, which isn't easy considering the situations and emotions she describes are far from my experience.

When she finally makes the first move by reaching over and taking one of my clammy hands in hers, staring at me with a clear and unmistakable, sloe-eyed look dripping with desire, I find myself stunned, my heart leaping in my chest like a caged animal. I know what's up, but I have a hard time believing the incredible luck of my fantasy beginning to come true: I've seen both *The Graduate* and *Summer of '42*, you know, and my anticipation rises to a fever pitch as she suggests we go into the small living room.

The hints and suggestions and turns of phrase she has used up to this point should have made things clear to me, and yet I have sat through it all dumbly, as though I've lost all ability to reason, as though my finely honed sense of observation—I considered becoming a journalist, remember, another half-baked idea if there ever was one—has left me in the lurch.

In hubris I'd like to believe she has fallen madly in love or some other ridiculous romantic notion, but let's face it: She's been drinking white wine the whole time instead of the coffee she'd promised, and now she's full-on drunk. Not me, though. Even if I was, the hormones squirting into me would knock it right out, just as they have the modest weed buzz I received from Jamie's earlier generosity.

We go into the living room and sit on the couch—it's a cozy little apartment, doesn't feel like we're in a motel. She turns on the TV to the *Tonight Show* but leaves the sound down, Carson standing in front of the multi-colored curtains and doing his monologue.

Sheila leans back and drapes her arm behind me on the couch, continuing her recitation of loneliness and betrayal. She tells me once again of her husband's hurtful infidelities, of years lost and time wasted. I tell her how sorry I am, how shitty people can be.

After a brief moment of hesitation—I can see her wheels turning—she leans into me; our lips meet, awkward at first, then with hunger. I get hot all over, sweating as though it is July and not March, a fever of young lust racing through my blood as if I've been given an intravenous injection of boiling water.

The light is low—she's thrown a towel over the lamp—but even still, when we pull away from each other's mouths, I can't help but see the age in her face. Far from being turned off, though, I feel as though this is another lucky turn of the wheel for me. I nevertheless think of Jamie a little bit, what she is doing, and I wonder if she's as lonesome as Sheila.

"I don't know if we should be doing this," Sheila announces as a brief flash of emotion crosses her face, a look somewhere between regret and fear. I am, after all, quite a young man.

"I don't see what's wrong with it."

Her next actions belie the uncertainty. She runs her hand up and down my stomach, closer and closer to ground zero, which is jutting upward, threatening to burst through the fly of my brown Levi's corduroys. I feel a certain pressure, like a volcano about to erupt upwards out of the crusty mantle that is my relative inexperience. The back of her hand nudges against that certain tent-pole; she and I both respond with a single, universally understood syllable:

"*Oh.*"

Events become a blur of pulled-off clothing, fumbling and groping as we move towards the small bedroom, the sheer want coming off Sheila's body in waves. Nola-Marie was always a little pudgy and soft, yes, but Sheila's voluptuous figure is different, her breasts and hips full, warm, and enveloping. Her bed frame squeaks as she pulls me on top of her.

She reaches down, tugging. I feel hard enough to drill through granite. My heart pounds as I finger the wet paradise between her thighs, with a smell so different from that of Nola-Marie: rich and earthy, the pheromones driving straight into my brain like the powerful drugs they are.

"You have a wonderful penis."

"Got it half price at a swap meet."

"Come to me, sweetheart."

My legs shaking and a certain pressure building inside me, one I hope I can hold off, I move on top and she guides me toward the Promised Land.

"Feels good as new." She sighs as I enter her, slick and wide compared to my previous experience with such activities. "It's been so long."

She is blazing on the inside; it is like sliding into hot pudding. Her hips thrust upward to meet my own tentative movements, something Nola-Marie never once did. My own ex had lain prone beneath my ministrations, acting as though she were doing me a favor.

I gasp as Sheila pulls my mouth to hers and wraps her legs around me. "You better hold on, wait, oh—"

I thrust a few times; she meets each one. As I feel her cool heels on the backs of my thighs, I twitch and spasm and explode, my cheeks now hot with shame instead of lust. Approximately twenty-six seconds have elapsed since penetration.

"Oh *baby*." She laughs, grabbing my buttocks and continuing to buck upwards against me. "Keep going."

"I'm, I'm *sorry*," I say in a horrified whisper, knowing full well that this woman—this grown woman—is laughing at me. But then a funny thing happens: as Sheila and I continue to kiss, and I perceive the lush, fertile body beneath mine, I realize I'm still as hard as before, and so I do as she asks: I keep going, and going, and going some more.

✸

THE LIGHT of the morning creeps through the shoddy drapes in Sheila's room, her window treatments no better than my own. I take in the drab surroundings, a three-room "suite" that is not much better than the rest of the dump, only that Sheila's apartment has personal effects and decorating touches that the other rooms don't have, as well as a small, galley kitchen versus the minuscule kitchenette tucked away in a corner of my room.

"Hey, sugar," I whisper as she rolls over towards me with a look of half-horror, half-embarrassment.

"Oh my god," she says, covering her face. "My makeup—!"

When I kiss her, our morning breath intermingling in a manner that is less unsavory than delightful to me—a kind of intimacy I've never known until this moment—she melts in my arms. Another hard-on, albeit a sore one, surges upwards against her soft thigh with a sudden and assured purpose in life.

Our lips pull apart with a smack. "You are a machine, Mr. Ray."

"The advantages of youth, my dear."

We fondle and grope and my fingers slip inside her and she moans and pulls me to her. "Hh, wait—I have to pee first." We both giggle and kiss some more until a knock, forceful, quick, officious, comes at her front door.

"Oh, for heaven sakes," she says, glancing over at the clock. "It's barely seven."

"Let's ignore it."

She reaches down for me. I wonder if she will again take me in her mouth as she had a few hours earlier, another new experience that left me breathless.

Her annoyance, and my incipient excitement, turns to astonishment and worry when a voice follows the knock, a deep growl that nevertheless attempts tenderness, and contrition: "Sheila, baby? I'm sorry about last night. You in there?"

"Oh no—it's *Carl.*"

"Your husband? Ex-husband, I mean?" My tumescent rod of love transforms into the form of a slippery eel that's anything but electric.

"Quick, quick," she whispers. "Go and get—no, stay here, I'll get your stuff out of the living room. Be quiet, don't say a word. He's really jealous."

"Super."

She scurries into the front living room, jiggling and bouncing as I scramble into my boxers, visions racing through my mind of Carl the ex-cop pummeling my Tillman Falls, teenaged pansy-ass into the wet beach sand.

Sheila tosses my clothes in the bedroom and snatches up a robe as Carl continues to knock and plead from outside. She slams the bedroom door with a wide-eyed look she compliments with a pleading, shushing finger to her lips.

"Quiet," she explains as though I don't understand. "I don't want to hurt his feelings."

And now I realize the relationship with her exe may be as complicated as mine is with Nola-Marie.

As I pull on my jeans and T-shirt, Sheila and her ex-husband embark on a tearful and angry conversation on the other side of the door.

I go over to the window that faces the alleyway—what a great view for the owner's suite!—and attempt to slide it open with only a modicum of noise. It sticks, and I force it with my elbow. When it finally comes loose, it does so with a dry, screeching sound, a window that hasn't been opened since winter's end.

I freeze in terror; I can hear they've stopped talking on the other side of the paper-thin walls. I don't so much hear as feel Carl's deep voice rumble, "What the heck was that?"

I don't wait for Sheila's answer. I slide through the window and drop the eight feet or so to the ground, hurting my ankle. It's going to be a long day at the Pavilion, I realize, as I hobble toward my room.

Coming around the corner I run into a sleepy-eyed Jamie standing outside my door.

"Hey, I came by later on last night," she says. "You went out without me?"

"I—well. I passed out at a party down the block," trying to smile. "Wow. What a time."

"But ya didn't come get me." She gives me a pouty expression, followed by a wink. "Me all by my lonesome?"

Everything's coming up Ray-Ray, I think. An embarrassment of riches. "What about tonight after I get off? You up for something?"

"Hey—want to catch a wake and bake, maybe some breakfast?"

"A capital idea, my lady." It would be prudent anyway, I think, to make myself scarce for a while. I can still smell Sheila all over me though; I wonder if Jamie can too. "Let me grab a quick shower first."

A FEW MINUTES LATER, I come out of my room to get Jamie only to see an older man standing beside the pool, looking forlorn into the gray-green Atlantic, the surface dappled and brilliant from the reflection of the springtime sun. I've only heard his voice, but something tells me this figure is Sheila's estranged ex-spouse.

Waiting out here for me.

Oh-shit-he-knows. I need to skedaddle.

Carl Wilson—a different sort of Beach Boy—has his meaty hands jammed into the pocket of his red Members Only jacket; a smoldering cigarette dangles from his lip, a long ash blown off by a gust of wind from the ocean. He's no boy—stocky, a head taller than me, thick but not fat. His broad shoulders remind me of my own father's.

A man. A real man. I had no business doing what I was doing with the woman he still cares about so much; it's possible I deserve what's coming to me.

Looking lost, he takes his hands out of his pockets and holds them up much as one would when conversing or arguing a point, as though on the losing end of yet another argument with God. I feel sorry for him, much as a nineteen-year-old can for a dude over twice his age.

Sorry, guilty, naughty—and scared. That's what I'm working with here.

Carl turns to go, finally, and we exchange a look—blue, piercing cop-eyes. I feel a stab of panic and wonder what was said between him and Sheila.

Pleasantries. I jam my hands into the pockets of my jeans. Hope I'm not blushing.

"You here with your family, son?"

"No, sir. I'm on my own. Work over at the Pavilion."

"Where you from?"

I half expect him to pull out one of those notebooks into which cops write down details of the crime scene. "Columbia. Well—by way of Tillman Falls. I'm a refugee from Southeastern."

"A refugee—meaning what?"

"I needed some time. An adventure, maybe." Mumbling and inarticulate, I sound like an idiot. "Get my head on straight."

Carl laughs and lights a fresh Camel. "I never had to go looking for any adventures myself."

"No?"

"My dad was a cop, like me," he says in a wistful Southern voice. "Like I used to be."

"Miss it?"

"Hell, no. Hell yeah. Oh, god—" Twin plumes of smoke issue from his nostrils and are swept away by the persistent breeze. "I sound like some bitter old man. Don't listen to another word."

"I get it. The passage of time. All things must pass. Whole bit."

"It's just—I seem to miss a lot these days." He squints at the wind-whipped, peeling paint of the Grand Strand. "Miss people I've lost. Absent friends."

I lift an imaginary flute of champagne. "To absent friends."

He chuckles. "Sure, kid. But go back to school, before you lose the taste for it altogether. Like I did."

"All in good time. Just want to make certain I'm on the right path."

"Let me know if you figure out what that is. Because on some days, even an old fart like me is still trying to figure it out." Carl pitches his butt into the sand along the walkway and trudges down the alley beside the motel.

After a painful duration, I let out a pent-up breath. If Carl knew what I'd been doing only hours before, I doubt he'd have been quite as cordial. Here's hoping Sheila knows how to keep a secret.

4

———

WEREWOLVES OF LONDON

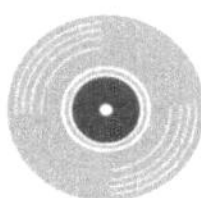

My stoney buzz makes the work go by like playtime in the bright sunshine. Pushing the broom, slinging the mop, tying up the trash bags, shooting the shit with the carnies and the custodians—it all seems like fantasy land amidst the rides and the cotton candy and the people whose only purpose during their wonderful week on vacation is to forget their normal, humdrum lives for a fleeting series of moments. And many of them perhaps thinking:

Were it only possible, yes, to live such a life all the time! If only.

But someone has to work, though. Otherwise—well, this whole civilization of ours will crumble, right? Someone's got to push the mop. Someone's got to serve up the slop. Being duly employed these last days has taught me much. I knew finally getting a job other than raking leaves and pine straw would make a man out of me. Sort of. This seems like too much fun though.

A lark. A laugh.

I have to remind myself the other people doing this work do not have a choice. And it is then I feel guilty and foolish. I try to shrug it off, though. Pretend I'm involved in some worthwhile enterprise. Proving myself.

Yeah—that's what I'm doing.

Near the end of my second full week, Pugliesi hears me working out with the *Monty Python* voices, and my low country old-money buffoon I call Ravenel Beaufain, a resident South of Broad down in *Chawwwwwwl-ston*, and then redneck Good Old Boy, and finally the Andy Kaufman foreign-man schtick, which invariably concludes with his signature catch-phrase: *Tank you veddy much.* I see the boss watching out of the corner of his eye as I have two other custodians in stitches. The black women from tiny, poor towns forty miles away in the Pee Dee think I'm the craziest young'un they've ever heard.

"He funny as them people on TV," Natasha says through a snort.

Her companion, Eunice, agrees with a kind smile. "He a hoot."

The three of us stiffen as Pugliesi strolls by and makes his presence known, telling the women to finish the ladies room and then they can go.

He takes me aside. "You like, what—some comedian? That what-a you are?"

My cheeks burn. "No, just having a goof, s'all."

"A goof?"

"I like to make people laugh. Wouldn't want to do it for a living though."

"Oh, sure—show business? It's brutal. A cousin of mine? Shot himself in the head when he didn't make it on-a the Broadway." He sneers, doing a light-in-the-loafers pirouette with an exaggerated, wide-eyed grin that dissolves into a scowl. "Left a note. It said if he couldn't be famous, he didn't wanna live." He spits onto the asphalt. "That's crazy."

"That's tough. Man—I'd just find something else to do." I'm reminded of this song by these new wave cats from New York called Talking Heads, about a couple who start writing TV shows since they love TV so much. "On the other hand, if your work isn't what you love," I quote from the lyrics, "then something isn't right."

Pugliesi seems pleased. "Smart boy. Just like I thought."

"I don't want to be famous, or anything like that. I want to..." I trail off, a harsh reminder of the reasons I'm here in the first place. "Do work I like. That part's important."

"No doubt."

But what *do* I like? What am I good at doing? Haven't a clue, haven't a clue, like the refrain of an annoying song I can't get out of my head. "Maybe I'll figure it out one day."

"You like pushing a broom?"

I shrug. "Honest work, bossman."

"You like doing them funny voices?"

I'm confused about the direction he's going, and I answer with caution, "I guess."

"Come with me, kid."

●

THE DUNKING BOOTH sits at an angle near one of the park entrances, in a prime spot designed to attract those with dollars burning holes in their pockets, the cash earmarked to be thrown away on trifles and momentary thrills either judiciously chosen or otherwise.

Jenkins calls such funds "walking around money," as in, *Mama, may I have some walking around money? I need to buy prophylactics before my date with Nola-Marie.* Those turkeys can have each other—as a matter of record, they can formally kiss my dimpled butt.

"Thing is," Pugliesi says, rubbing his hard gut and grimacing, "Rivers is about to get 'let go', as they say."

Rivers, as I've learned, is the dunking booth clown, a bleary-eyed, pudgy guy of indeterminate age. Booze-hounding since the end of last season, as rumors suggest, has made him unreliable. Seems after he split up with his woman, he took a precipitous turn for the sullen.

Mr. George informed me in hushed detail that the dunking booth clown's girlfriend ran off with a wealthy man from Florida who owned a waterslide park, and "poor Mr. Rivers can't," George says words like *cahn't* and *Auhnt* British-style, "seem to get over the loss."

"The clown's heart—it's broken."

"Some men," he concluded with a grave air, which made me wonder if Mr. George had had first hand experience, "don't always recover from a lost, great love."

Furthermore, there's talk that money went missing after a particularly busy night at the park a week ago, and it may have had something to do with Rivers, who's been especially morose and inebriated all week.

All Pugliesi says, though, is: "He's ready for retirement from the old insult factory. He's lost his pep—his 'joey da vee', as the frogs say."

"He has seemed introspective and depressive for a dunking booth clown. To deliver the sort of hectoring that the job requires. And all."

Pugliesi stares through me. "Say what?"

I roll back the college-boy act a bit. "Leastways, since I been working here. He ain't seemed too happy. And all."

"No, he's not. He's got problems. It's a real shame, that Rivers. Last night, he swore in-a front of a group of little girls. We can't have it. This is a family park. You understand?"

"Indubitably so."

I tend to eschew the SAT-fueled wordplay—I scored 780 on verbal, not so good on the math side—as much as possible with working people like Pugliesi, or just about everyone except maybe Chris. Often I adopt a patois more suited to the person with whom I'm communicating, and I find the exchange goes much smoother. I believe Ray the thesaurus king—perhaps another mere vocal affectation, I think—tends to make folks suspicious, sometimes, of my motivations. So, I tone it down, I try to blend in, I try to come off like one of the guys and not some college boy. Not to be manipulative, or anything, but it helps get what you want if the person you want it from thinks that you're *one of them* versus just *them*—the other, the outsider. Come to mention it, that's the way I approach my own family, in conversation sounding less like myself—whatever that means—than I do them.

"Rivers did perk up a bit the other night while giving some guy the business about his sandals and dark socks. Man, that rube didn't hit the target once in six tries."

"That's the thing. With this game, the madder you make 'em, more likely they are to miss, and you? You stay high and dry while still making the green stuff, eh? You know you get a cut of the take in this job, don't-cha?"

"Sure, sure," I say, lying. "I could use more money."

"You think you could do all them funny voices, that Limey stuff, in the booth?"

I'm stunned. "Would this be considered a promotion, Mr. Pugliesi?"

He laughs and drapes his arm around me, giving me a whiff of Old Spice and smoker's breath. "Sure, kid. Whatever you want to call it. A promotion for the college boy already. If you wanna call it that."

STONED, Jamie and I loll around on the bed, the waves crashing against the shore while we watch daytime television. I get up and stretch; Jamie and I have become quite, *ahem,* close in the interim since her abandonment.

She is not Nola-Marie, nor is she Sheila; what Jamie is, though, is a little firecracker—she's wearing me out.

Who am I kidding? I could get used to being worn out.

Speaking of my erstwhile mature lover, with whom I now have a strained and embarrassed relationship, I get up and squint through the curtains as Sheila, dressed in a nice lime-green pant suit and with her hair done and makeup just-so, walks around with a small group of business types in casual suits of plaid and earth tones.

Two of the men remove their jackets and roll up their shirtsleeves in the early spring warmth. They stand with their hands on their hips and seem extremely pleased. One of them fiddles with his tie and speaks with animation. He holds his arms up toward the sky; the other men look upward as well, nodding with satisfied smiles. They each in turn shake hands with Sheila, who keeps an odd smile frozen on her face. She's nowhere near as pleased as her suited companions, but doesn't want to show it.

I turn off the TV and re-start the cassette I bought over at the Myrtle Square Mall the other day. *"Ah-ooooh, ah-ooooh,"* Zevon sings from the boom-box.

Jamie stretches and gives me what I have come to term "the look." I respond by leaping onto the bed. I growl and paw at my new girlfriend like a lascivious, ravenous beast. She's so different from both of my previous lovers. That's what I get to call them now, ex-lovers, this growing list of my amorous encounters.

But Jamie, when I look into her almond-shaped eyes, I think I could fall for her, and in spite of a few flaws. She has acne scars on her cheeks; her nose is not just upturned, but a little crooked; her hips are kind of big underneath her hippie dresses and jeans. She's no Southern debutante like Nola-Marie, but that makes Jamie a kind of goddess to me, as real as the days are becoming long now that the clocks have been changed to Daylight Savings Time.

But the reverie, and my nascent erection, are shattered as Boosey puts through a call to my room from someone with a heavy Jersey accent who says angrily, "Where the fuck is my girl, asshole?"

This must be Lars. I'm going to kick that Boosey's butt later—he's been snickering at me all week about Jamie. "She gets around, don't she?" he whispered, leering.

As I hand her the phone, my heart pounds in my ears. With wide eyes and spots of color in her cheeks, Jamie speaks to Lars for about five minutes as I hang in the doorway, trying to be polite. The name Paco comes up a few times; Jamie seems more concerned about this Paco character than Lars.

After she hangs up she tells me he's going to wire her money to take the bus home. That's he's scored some more grass, big time, and he misses her terribly and is angry about whoever answered the phone, and if she doesn't come back home, he's going to do something rash, nasty, painful.

"Well," I say in my *outrageous* French voice, "this eez *terrrrible* news." I'm not as light-hearted about it all as I might seem, however. In fact, I'm downright jealous.

She sits on the edge of the bed, pensive, rocking back and forth in her t-shirt and panties. I see with perfectly lucid and intelligent eyes that she's weighing the options: summer in South Carolina with a janitor-*cum*-dunking booth clown, or back home to familiar turf with a boyfriend who, if what he hints at is true, might soon be rolling in bread.

Many possibilities race through my mind in the seconds after she's rung off with Lars, most of which cause little pinpricks of cold pain and fear in my chest. She's never looked lovelier, my hippy girl with dirty feet and a smile as fresh as a field of sunflowers; that I will lose her is, I suspect, a foregone conclusion, and, oh, does it make me mad, the flowers replaced by a brown field of brittle, dying weeds.

"Well?"

She bites her lip. "Says he's already wired me the money. Alls I got to do is hit up the Western Union."

"And?"

"I told him I'd pick it up this afternoon. The money," she clarifies, as though I've got the shortest memory in history.

"Great."

"But that doesn't mean I've decided to go back." A slow smile spreads across her face. "If he sends enough," she giggles, *"I'll* pay next week's rent."

She kisses me emphatically, her tongue probing with lust at my own. Warren Zevon howls and we lose another hour within each other, the warm salt of the evaporating ocean settling across our bodies grown flushed and damp with passion.

◦

"I've got some bad news," Sheila says, her cheeks red. Her voice comes so small I can barely hear her. "I've wanted to talk to you all week anyway."

"I say, madam, you're going to have to speak up if you wish me to hear you properly," I reply in upper-class twit.

"You and your voices."

In anticipation of my debut in the booth on Saturday, I've been practicing various accents all week, mostly to myself. I will have to refine my style to include the necessary taunting to inflame the passions of passersby, if I wish to be a success at this new profession of mine. Normally, I wield my humor in gentle ways, but this new job will require a bit more badgering, mean-spirited or otherwise, in the mix.

"Here's the news. You might as well plan on finding somewheres else to live, kiddo."

My heart flutters, a tad broken. The fantasies of further encounters with the buxom Sheila have already been tempered by subsequent events, obviously, but I still feel a small twinge of rejection. She'd already made clear what a mistake our encounter was—albeit a lovely one, she has emphasized.

"I don't understand," I say in a voice that sounds like that of a little boy, instead of a man. "I thought you said, until the season kicks in."

"Things have changed."

"Is it Jamie?"

"It's not that, Ray. I'll always," she begins to whisper, "remember our special night. Our *special* night," she repeats and places a tender, warm hand on my forearm.

"I kind of hoped we'd have another," I say in the small voice, suddenly feeling stupid for even having verbalized such a thought.

"No—*no*, honey. I feel like I took advantage of you. I have a son your age, for heaven's sake." A sad smile, then: "That Jamie's a lucky girl. I wouldn't—well."

"What?"

"Just be careful about getting your heart broken, Ray. She went awfully easily from that other guy to you. Don't you think?"

"Hey, it's the beach. No sweat. Just having fun."

"Well, I care about you, that's all. Want you to be careful."

Her motherly advice hangs in the air and makes me feel squeamish—a gentle nudge of Oedipal discomfort, maybe, although I can tell you that my own mother is no Sheila Wilson, that's for good-god-damn sure. My mother looks like, well, someone's mother. Sheila, on the other hand, is a ripe, fecund goddess. I hope her sexy, musky scent stays with me forever.

I stand mute before her, shrugging in response.

"The thing is—I signed the papers yesterday. Those people who've been around?"

"I've seen them."

"Did okay, too. Not as much as you dream about, but still—more than enough to move on, start over." She frowns, shakes her head just so, a touch of seller's remorse, one presumes, for a most fleeting of instants.

"That's that."

"One last season, well, it turned out that was last year's. But it's for the best," she concludes without sounding certain.

I perceive the passage of time with even more *gravitas* than I did with Carl. Maybe these two should get back together after all.

"It's not so bad. You seem tired of it all, Sheila. Can I say that?"

"It don't offend me none, sugar." She starts to reach over for my hand, but stops herself. "So how's this new girlfriend?"

My cheeks flame. "Hey—we're just friends."

"So I heard when I was walking down the alleyway earlier. Real close friends, sounds like."

I feel as busted as the time Mom came bursting through my bedroom door with a load of clean laundry while I was hunched over in the act of scrutinizing one of Larry Flynt's prestigious publications. I don't know what to say. "I'm so sorry, Sheila—it just happened."

"Oh, lord—all you men say that, don't you?" She laughs. "I'll help you find a place to stay, okay?"

"You will?"

"Let me call a couple folks."

"Thanks."

She looks back and winks. "Ain't gonna be oceanfront, though."

"A fleeting extravagance to be fondly remembered. I'm—I'm in your debt, beautiful," I growl in a passable Bogart. "We'll always have Ocean Boulevard."

Wistful as can be: "Here's looking at you, kid."

I watch as she sashays toward the office. It is only then that I realize Carl is sitting there in his Oldsmobile. He's been watching us the whole time, and I'm mortified all over again, exposed and halfway frightened yet again that *he knows*. Surely not!

She turns back to me and says with a naughty smile, "Tell me something: Was I your first?"

How to answer? A gentle lie. "Yeah. Yeah, you were."

She seems pleased. "I wouldn't have thought so, Mr. Ray. Not as good as you were."

"Thanks, doll. My pleasure." I offer her a small bow, and she goes to her ex-husband. Carl stares at me with hard eyes that glint in the bright sunshine.

◦

So now Jamie gets the money from Western Union—a hundred bucks, a decent score—and the next day she ponies up for the first week at the one-bedroom apartment Sheila finds for us. It's about three blocks off the beach in a rundown, over-and-under duplex about as far on the other side of the Olympic Flame as I was at Sheila's place. It's not the best, but it's still within reasonable walking distance to all the action.

We go back to the motel to get the rest of our stuff together—our stuff, how romantic—but I just about shit when I see the car in the gravel parking lot: Dad. Dad's gray Caddy—he calls it the Shark.

This is going to be bad. How the fuck did he find me?

I send Jamie around the other side through the alley while I make a beeline for the office. As I approach, I can see the my father's ample silhouette through the tinted glass; he is leaning against the counter on one elbow, in that relaxed posture he adopts when he's talking to the ladies at the Colonial Cup in between placing bets on the horse races and quaffing Schlitz Malt Liquor tallboys.

I decide that part of being a mature adult is confronting adversity rather than running from it, so I boldly go where no DeKalb hath dared before.

"Why, *fahthur*," I drawl, "Lord have *mercy*. Who's running the household back home? Surely you haven't left Pitty Pat in charge again! Not after last time. Oh, it was dreadful, the biscuits were burned and—"

"Enough!" His face, open and pleasant only seconds before, is a purple mask of fury. His stance is that of a solid prizefighter, holding his hands up at me in two half-fists. He extends a finger in my direction, but addresses Sheila:

"Ma'am," he says in controlled politeness that betrays a strained underpinning of anger, "would you mind awfully much excusing my son and me for just a moment?"

Now Sheila is the mortified party. Her huge eyes meet mine. She shoots me a look as though we're both in trouble.

I give her a small wave—*it's okay*.

"Yes, sir, Mr. DeKalb. I'll be in the back if you need anything." Halfway through the curtain she adds, "Your son is a fine young man. I haven't met many like him." Her quick smile at me—a secret smile—almost quells the dread that's settling into my gut.

Daddy Dick ignores her. "Now look here, you little shit-ass." He takes a step toward me, the vein in his forehead pulsing.

"Dad," I say in my normal voice for once, "let's do this outside. It's a beautiful day."

"I don't give a good god-durn if it's the first day of spring or the first blizzard in hell. Have you lost your *mind*, son? Your mother—" He stops himself, his lips working up and down. "Your mother's fit to be tied."

I feel a great wave of empathy for the old man. My actions are putting him through a nightmare with her, as loudly and demonstratively protective as she is with regard to her young'uns—which is yet another problem from which I seek escape. "Come on out here, Dad."

We shuffle along together toward the beach, Dad huffing and puffing while I offer a number of vain attempts at placation to his injured sense of filial loyalty. He is more than dissatisfied—he is sputtering and seething with ire.

"Now, I let this go on longer than I should have, boy, in the hope that you'd come around on your own. I see it ain't working too well."

"Doesn't look that way."

I see Jamie peeking out the window; I wave her off and give a discreet thumbs up, my hand held low down by my hip. That I don't feel much like introducing her to Dad is no reflection on her—only on him.

"You ain't telling me a grown boy like yourself thinks it's a good idea to throw away a semester of college."

"I'm not sure I was getting your money's worth out of it."

"What makes you think it's up to you in the first place? You writing the god-durn checks?"

The truth is I had a small scholarship the first year, but after my grades fell below an acceptable level, Dad indeed found himself footing the tuition and board—as if a couple of thousand dollars was a huge burden for him. Southeastern's only about five or six hundred a semester for in-state students. I'll fucking pay for it myself if I decide to go back.

"I'll fucking pay for it myself if I decide go back," I retort.

"Son, don't you dare curse at me like that. You hear me?"

"Hell, no, I don't hear you, *Dick*."

His hand shoots out and slaps me across the mouth, hard.

"Hey—!" I stagger back, stunned. He's never so much as raised a paw at me in the past. That's mother's job, like the time they came home drunk and found me in the same condition, catching me red-handed putting back a mostly-empty quart of bourbon into the liquor cabinet. I never knew if she hit me out of anger over my being drunk, or the fact that I had killed the best part of her stash.

My eyes sting with water like they did when she clocked me a good one, tears of either shame or surprise, I suppose. "Fuck you," I squawk in a high-pitched voice. All I can think is that Jamie just saw me get slapped like a petulant child. I'm humiliated.

Dick DeKalb looks shocked by his actions. Perhaps what runs through his head is what any politician would worry about: being seen striking a child in public—his own kid, no less.

"Boy, I swear you make me so durn mad."

"Daddy, you ain't never hit me in your life."

"C'mon."

"C'mon where?"

"Just get in the car."

"No."

"I ain't gonna hogtie you and take your skinny butt home—although I ought to. Let's go get something to eat and hash this out before either of us does anything else stupid."

•

MAMMY'S KITCHEN UP on the King's Highway is quiet as we sit and eat our breakfast. "Ain't hardly a soul around here," Dick remarks.

"Doesn't get cranked up again until May, they tell me."

"Who's they?"

"The lady at the motel—and my boss."

Dick pauses with a forkful of Denver omelet halfway to his mouth. He sits blinking, stunned. I haven't worked for anything in my life up until this point. "Who's your 'boss'?"

"This guy, Pugliesi, over at the Pavilion."

My dad starts laughing. "The Pavilion? Like, right over yonder?" He turns and gestures out the window at the roller coaster, which is, of course, idle since the park is closed during the week. He scoffs and laughs some more as he chews his eggs with amused aplomb.

"Yeah. They brought me on as a janitor, but I'm already on the way up."

But now the slab of egg and cheese becomes caught in my father's throat. He coughs and sputters and finally swallows the food. He draws in a great lungful of breath—he really was choking, it seems—and quickly drains half his water glass with a grimace. He doesn't have the foreknowledge of how salty the tap water is in this town—it's a bit of shock at first. Makes you wish they sold bottled, distilled water in the vending machines instead of cold Coke-Colas.

"A janitor? Son, what are you, one of them black boys who rakes the yard? Or are you a DeKalb? Jesus *Christmas!*"

"Daddy, shut up, for god sakes."

"Son, I really am worried about you. All this mess, now, I understand what it's like to want to run around. I know I don't seem like it, but at your age I was more like you than I was Jenkins."

"He'd be crushed to hear you say that."

"Well, he always was the sensitive type. Between you, me and the salt shaker, he's got a long row to hoe before we can run him for a statewide office. But there's time to get him seasoned. Just like there's time for you, too."

I'm sipping coffee and pushing around my half-eaten Belgian waffle in its lukewarm bath of thin syrup. I was also gnawing on half a sausage link but bit into something gritty, and since then my stomach has gone queasy. "Daddy—I'm glad you put it that way."

"Oh?"

"Uh-huh. If I got all this time, then why can't I do some living?"

"Well, son, you can, you can. What you think going off to college is supposed to be?"

"I'm not talking about school."

"I want to tell you something—you know what all it took for me to go to school? You have any idea-r at all?"

"I know, Daddy. It was tough. Money, et cetera."

"Well, I don't think neither one of you spoiled brats has any idear what it can be like. I mean—I don't want to sound like what your Mama and me have done for y'all you don't deserve, or nothin'—just that the sacrifice it took to get you here ain't something to discount, to take for granted. I barely made it through law school because I had to work so much to pay for it."

My dad's rarely been this philosophically spot-on, and I tell him so. I've always been a decent enough student of history. I know what granddad went through in the Depression and the big war that followed; after he got home, Benny DeKalb worked at a variety of blue-collar endeavors until his untimely death from heart disease a few years ago. How can you not be aware of this stuff, your past, your roots?

Daddy's right, though: Not everyone is cognizant of his own history, but I am. Maybe too aware, sometimes. Do I understand what it means? Maybe not, to hear him tell it. I tell him a version of all that, trying to soothe the beast.

"Well, good, good, I'm glad to hear you say you agree. Because you acting like the thousand dollars I done spent this year—for school, Ray, not for toys, for *college*—ain't got one lick a meaning to you."

Now I'm actually embarrassed at being called to the carpet on this point. Of course it has crossed my mind; but when you come from money, albeit one generation's worth, I guess you sometimes take it for granted. Now I feel selfish, childish. "I'm sorry, Daddy. I know I wasn't thinking straight about that part. But like I said, I'm going to pay for tuition myself when I go back. That's right."

"And when, pray tell, is that gonna be?"

"Oh, in the fall." A safe enough statement—autumn seems a century or more away. I'm not so old at nineteen that summers don't still stretch out a bit, at least when you allow them to. I took a summer session Econ course last year to make up for a dropped class in the spring, and before I knew it, the fall semester was underway. Summer school—fuck that noise. No wonder I need a break.

"That's half a durn year."

"Plenty of time for me to make some bread."

"Bread," he laughs. "You know your Mama's about as teed off as I ever seen."

"And you ain't?"

Dick wipes his mouth and gives me a friendly, old-timey Daddy smile, the kind I've become unaccustomed to seeing since our relationship has soured in the last couple of years. "I've always known you was a smart boy, Raymond. Smarter than you let on sometimes."

"That why you call me a little smart-ass all the time?" I give him a wink.

"Now, now, son. You know what I mean. That's—that's why we're all so *shocked* by this."

"I've had a rough year."

"I know, and now—with Nola-Marie and Jenkins—well." His face reddens at this reference to the sordid romantic triangle having sprung up between his boys.

If you add in Jamie, does that make it a trapezoid? Oh, hell—has the year really been that bad? Or am I just a drama queen?

"I just need some time to sort things out." I change to a tried and true voice, part Groucho, part kvetching Jewish old-timer: "Why I picked this particular place, *ack*," I gesture around at the tourist town outside the restaurant windows, "we'll *nev-ah* know."

"You got that part right." Now he's dead serious again. "So you're coming home with me today, right?"

I roll my eyes. "I can't. I just signed a lease on a place through the season. I'm gonna live and work down here, hit the beach, give myself some space. Yep: That's what I'm gonna do." I am trying to convince myself as much as I am him.

He shakes his head, the wattle underneath his chin jiggling. He smacks his thick lips and says *mm-mm-mm.* "I come back without your ass, and Mama's gonna skin me."

"Well, we're gonna find out what you look like on the inside, then." I fold my arms and lean back, locking eyes in assured defiance.

It is a long moment as we sit facing each other over our now room-temperature breakfast entrées. But it is a standoff I win, even if I must still give some ground:

"You can forget them trust fund checks, boy. I tell you that much."

"That's okay," I lie in mild consternation. "I'm sure all you have to do is say the word and that'll stop toot-sweet." I know I have him there—this is old money from Mama's side, to whom the DeKalbs had at first seemed like crude interlopers, according to my grandmother, at least.

"Don't play me. You know that—"

"—I was Grandmama's favorite?"

Dick sits with his mouth turned inside out, shaking his head and gazing out the window at the light traffic only yards away, the signal cycling through its interminable green-yellow-red pattern. I wonder what is going through his head, whether he's thinking about what a sleepy, small town Myrtle Beach seems right now, how other than the ocean and the amusement parks it doesn't look any more exciting than downtown

Tillman Falls on a Saturday night. I myself have had this feeling; he confirms it with his next words.

"Son—I know this is the beach, and all, but I c'ain't understand how this could be more interesting than going to Southeastern. That was all you talked about for the longest time, wa'n't it?"

I finish my coffee and set the chipped cup down with a *clunk* that is louder than I expected. "People change."

He seems bemused by this remark, his face a pink mask of skepticism and seeming foreknowledge, the kind you don't share with someone you'd rather see take a fall. "Ain't the first time someone told me that. Still waiting to see it happen, though." He snaps a bill out of his money clip and slides it under his plate without waiting for the check.

Outside on the cracked sidewalk, he fires up a cigarette and looks down the street at the junction of 501 and 17, at the old movie theatre across the way. I follow his gaze: the new-looking Pavilion signage on the corner, the Maryland Fried Chicken joint across the street. A van-load of teenagers driving too fast, surfboards lashed to the top of their rattling, throaty Dodge, blow past us hooting and hollering.

"Last chance," he says through a wet belch and a lungful of smoke. "You come home, and all's forgotten."

"Hard bargain. But I done said *mah* piece," I reply in hillbilly-ese. "I got to git on back, now, pardner. I got to do for me and *mine*."

He wants to try again, I can see it on his face. I'm not unsympathetic—indeed, I can well envision the hell he's going to go through once he shows back up in the midlands with the grim reportage regarding my lack of acquiescence to his demands. "Well, son, I hope you find what you're looking for."

"When I do, you'll be the second to know."

He fixes me with a cold-eyed stare. "Don't call me, though, the first time you get into trouble. You understand? You want to be a man, you work through whatever happens. I'm serious now. You want to learn some lessons? You do it on your own here this summer."

"Don't worry, old man, that's the *idea-r*," I mock. I give him the heartiest handshake I can muster, but my own hand still feels as small inside his great mitt as it always has.

We part then, but only after, in an odd, awkward moment, he gets the money clip back out and peels off two hundred dollars, which he thrusts at me. I start to beg off this generous gift, but a quiet voice whispers *the money might make all the difference.*

Upon a brief instant of reflection, though, a more stentorian tone breaks in: *He's giving you his blessing, nitwit. Run with it—it's some kind of miracle.*

And it is thus I bid my father adieu. I consider one last nonsensical thought as I watch him climbing into the Shark, a man whose hopes and dreams for me still seem monstrous in spite of my victory. As he runs a comb through his hair while checking himself in the rearview—it's something he does when he's nervous, the hair-combing—I think in a quite amused manner, *I saw a werewolf eatin' an omelet at Mammy's Kitchen; his hair was perfect!*

5

ACCIDENTALLY, LIKE A MARTYR

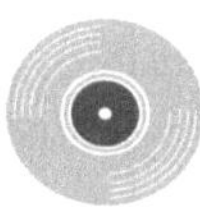

"**S**ay there, pal. Yeah—*you.*"

As April rolls along, a few Canadians still wander here and there, even though the big week for those folks was a month ago now. You can spot them by their doughy countenance and completely un-hip clothing—not that much different from people I grew up around, come to think of it. In my brief time inside the dunking booth cage, I've learned to suss out the easy mark, the family man with kids to impress, the strutting teenager with a pimply-faced female companion waiting to be dazzled.

"Oh no, fella. No, sir." These folks could be from Minnesota, I suppose, and not Canada, but to a Carolina boy like me their accent is just as exotic. "You're not hooking me in."

Pear-shaped and tall, he reminds me of the French comedian Jacques Tati. Chris took me to see one of those comedies at the student union last semester. It was funny, and didn't matter it wasn't in English. I appreciate good physical comedy; it translates well. Chris called the actor the French Chaplin, which didn't mean much to me. I enjoyed the movie for what it was—a gentle laugher about a guy on vacation at the beach.

This little dunking booth act is something altogether different from slapstick, however: This is a think-piece. This is verbal. Just me and the microphone and a little speaker hanging on the side of the cage. And the marks, of course, waiting to be sucked into my vortex of taunting.

I smile to myself. For someone not getting hooked in, the whole group of them has now stopped. "Say, your wife's real pretty, there, mister," I continue, mocking his accent perfectly. "Sure looks a little knock-kneed, though, if ya know what I mean." I don't in fact know what I mean; sometimes the words just have to sound funny to get a reaction.

"Say, now, fella…"

"Probably a bit like your mother too, I betcha. Uh-huh. Yessir."

In seconds, Tati is handing over a couple of carefully folded dollar bills to Maybelle, a corpulent, sour woman in her fifties who sits in a little freestanding, plywood ticket-booth, making change from a money belt and dispensing the baseballs—gray, battered objects culled from god knows where. Maybelle doesn't like me, won't look at me, won't talk to me. I wonder why; in my imagination I come to the conclusion that she is in love with Rivers (in spite of his flaws), and my having replaced him so easily really gripes her ass. I'm just conjuring up scenarios, though.

"I say, dear fellow," switching to a mellifluous British man of letters. "That's quite a remarkable family of bipeds whom you've been observed herding around these facilities, my good man. Yes yes, yes yes, I've seen these mutations quite often in my travels to Tierra Del Fuego and Tasmania. Piteous creatures, these. It will make a fascinating presentation to the adventurers' society." I chortle, causing a touch of feedback on the microphone. "*Most* exotic."

The mark, now more than fished in, has removed his burgundy windbreaker and handed it to an adolescent son, a freckled boy who is scowling at me in my fright wig, rainbow suspenders, and enormous sunglasses. The daughter, a flaxen-haired girl five or six years of age, seems delighted, giggling behind her hands. I lower the glasses just so and give her a conspiratorial wink. The wife, heavyset in her flip-flops and pedal pushers, is standing off to the side, rolling her eyes and smoking a Virginia Slims 100.

Jamie dressed me in my outlandish costume; she said I should try to evoke a zany Mork from Ork vibe. Can't quite pull off the Robin Williams rapid-fire manic bit, but the voices come quickly and easily enough that my delivery does have a scattershot—yes, zany, if you will—quality. Once I put the wig on I didn't feel nervous, and I knew then how it felt to play a role, which I'd always perceived myself as doing anyway. That wig fits like a glove, like it was made for me. I feel no buffoonery or self-consciousness, only newfound power at this novel form of anonymity. It is an odd sensation—but I dig it, man, I dig it.

"You're in for a quick soakin', fella, that's all I got to say to you." The guy squints, working his lips and gauging the target. He leans back, stiff, and in those seconds I know he's going to throw wild.

It's Sunday night, only the second of my two shifts in the cage thus far, but I've already settled into a real groove. At first I wondered if this comedy-in-a-cage bit isn't the "something" I should be doing—but then it really ticked me off the first time I got nailed and went into the water. Really, though, the job has come so easy it's spooky.

Last night, Pugliesi stood watching me work, stamping his feet and howling. He came over in between marks wiping tears out of his eyes. "You're a natural, college boy. A natural. Keep it a-clean is all. Just remember all the tender ears out here."

Sure enough, the scuffed baseball misses the target, only about eight inches across, by a solid foot. Not a big one, that round bullseye. The gray ball goes bouncing into the netting that hangs from the frame and rolls down into a basket.

I start hee-hawing into the mic, honking at the top of my lungs like a goose. Then, as though I am an old-timey carnival barker: "Step right up, ladies and gentlemen and youths alike. *See* as the *impaired* man *disappoints* his children and *embarrasses* his family while—"

Thok! And into the water I go with a splash. The tank is cold and nasty, the bath briny like the sea itself. I scramble to reset the seat and get back to the mic.

The small crowd now gathered cheers with glee, maybe a dozen people in flip-flops, shorts and jackets, several pink with sunburn. The mark holds his arms up in triumph, like Rocky Balboa. "I got one more to go, too, mister, how's that for ya, eh? Just, just you climb on back outta there, now." He and his son slap five, awkward, like it's the first time. Touching.

Within seconds I'm back on the mic—it's mounted just outside so I don't have to touch it and electrocute myself—and I charge right ahead. "Swing batter swing batter swing swing *sah*-wing. Step right up ladies and gentlemen, step right up and see the man *fail* to reproduce his winning throw!"

Everyone laughs. *Thok!* Splash.

Fuck—a live one. Ah, well.

"That'll teach ya to mess with a little league coach, guy." He winks and I give him a curt nod.

"Tank you veddy much." Everyone applauds as water drains down my legs into the Chuck Taylors. They needed a good washing anyway.

The dunking's not so bad. It's all in the job. I worry, at this rate, about getting a rash, though. Last night I barely got wet at all, maybe three times. Tonight, on the other hand? I'm getting pummeled. I can see how one's self esteem could suffer when up against an egregious run of eagle-eyed little league coaches.

One guy did get pretty mad last night. It was around ten-thirty, and I went a bit too far about his tarted-up redneck queen of a wife, speaking as I did of trailer parks and about a poor man's Tammy Wynette and big hair and all that. I did it in a condescendingly corn-pone accent—admittedly, probably not that far from what ought to be my own natural patois. I got him so riled up he missed all three of his tries at the target, only nicking it once. Afterwards he cursed with bitter invective and reached for his wallet, but then he and his spouse got into a screaming argument about him buying another three chances. He ended up marching over and smacking the cage right in front of my face and jabbing a finger at me.

"I oughta wait for your ass, boy. You ain't gonna be in there all night."

"I say, dear fellow, tsk tsk. You must be more gentle. *Ohm,*" I sang. "Chant with me, now."

I leaned back and held my hands in a gesture of prayerful repose as his wife dragged him away—but not until after she started calling me a queer and a butthole and every variation thereof.

I've done all right tonight, some decent bucks I think. This makes pushing the broom seem like a chump's deal. Pugliesi is a smart guy, recognizing talent like mine.

❋

JAMIE COMES and watches until things slow down, I get tired, and have a hard time hooking in the marks: They've blown their fun-money for the day, and enjoy my taunting for free, the cheapskates.

I observe her talking with a couple of guys, all three displaying furtive body language. I get distracted running a routine on someone, and when I look back over, she's vanished along with her new friends.

She shows back up about the time that we shut the booth down. I squish-squish into the bathrooms and change inside one of the odiferous stalls. The dry clothes are a welcome, comfortable relief—but even so, I sure could use some baby powder. My asshole feels chapped and itchy from sitting in wet britches for two nights in a row. Maybe I should get some rubber drawers to wear instead of my Fruit of the Looms.

Jamie's smoking a clove cigarette. I try to hold her hand but it's clammy and I let it go after about half a block. We walk by some younger kids outside of Ripley's Believe It Or Not, which is also closing down for the night. The group of teenagers, junior high age, start quietly chattering among themselves as we pass: They think the clove is grass.

"God-damn," one of the boys whispers in a flat accent I can't place, maybe Ohio. "They're smoking it right out on the street!"

"We could sling some of that weed to them," Jamie whispers. She's jittery and kind of nervous, I note, not like the laid-back Jamie I'm used to. "I got a few nickel bags on me."

I figured we'd just smoke through the rest of what she had for as long as we could. "We got bucks, babe."

I'm trying to be frugal, but for shits and giggles we went out the other night to an Italian joint called Villa Romana and stuffed ourselves—yeah, I blew some of the Daddy-money, but in spite of that momentary lapse in judgment, I'm determined to make it last.

"I know I know," she says with irritation. "But it won't last. And I don't expect to live off of you, dude."

I've discovered already that Jamie gets moody. After two weeks of cohabitation, I've already come to expect these pendulum-swings. Still— she likes to get down, even when she's got on one of her frowny faces. I've gone through a couple of boxes of Trojans already—she finally let me put it in there without one yesterday, and I really gave it to her for a while without worrying too awfully much about blowing my stack. I've gotten pretty damn good, like my screwing prowess has been some sort of innate but heretofore dormant ability. I guess that's the way it is for most everyone. No way to know. Who would I discuss it with? Dad? Jenkins? Christ—forget it.

Now my brother and I can compare notes about Nola Marie, though—he'll hate that part. At Thanksgiving, I'll be sure to ask him about the location and qualities of little moles and other intimate, identifying marks. It'll be a hoot.

"Give a hoot, don't pollute," I say out loud.

Jamie has the frowny-face on right now. "Huh?" She's sweating, licking her lips. I think I know what's going on here, and I don't like it. I've never been into anything much harder than grass, and I don't think it's a good idea for her, either. But who am I to say?

"Hey—non sequiturs are where it's at, babe. Read all about it in *People* magazine." I glance back to see the young kids following us about ten yards back, and as a group have quieted down considerably. I nudge her and move to cross in front of the Gay Dolphin, me pulling at her damp hand. Jaywalking through the holes in the traffic is easy enough, although it's pretty heavy for this late on a Sunday at this point in the spring. At least, that's what Pugliesi said: "Gonna be one great effing season, that's what I think, all-a this traffic so soon."

We continue down the block until there's a public access walkway between two motels. "Beach?"

She shrugs. "Why not."

Moody, this girl is. She's also on speed, or something, all twitchy. Never cared for speed.

"So where'd you go earlier?"

"When?"

"With those cats I saw you talkin' to."

She pulls her hand away. "Oh, god, you gonna start in too, like Lars? Men. Sheesh."

I try to put my arm around her. "Look here, li'l sister."

"Don't call me that." She pulls away and walks up ahead. She stops and takes her flip-flops off, the kind with the woven-footbed and soft, velvet straps. Her threadbare bellbottoms drag in the sand.

"Jamie—come on!"

She hurries on up toward a high-rise hotel's wooden walkway that ramps downward from the pool area to the loose white sand beyond the sea oats. I try to catch up, but she's really booking it, and by the time I get into the pool area Jamie has disappeared around the corner of the building, one of the tallest on the oceanfront. It's not that far to the parking lot and Ocean Boulevard beyond, but by the time I get there, my girlfriend— or whatever—is nowhere to be seen.

◦

AN HOUR later I'm sitting there in the apartment eating Fruity Pebbles and listening to Pink Floyd *Animals,* and then after that, the Zevon again. I've rolled up a doober out of the roaches left in the ashtray; Jamie seems to have kept all the weed either on her, or else well-hidden, which is stupid.

Unless she's keeping secrets from me.

I get a stab of panic, that little paranoia vibe you get sometimes while high, that moment of realization whereupon dreadful thoughts rudely announce themselves by bursting through the gentle repose of your buzz, shattering the mood, sometimes indelibly: *What if she's not coming back?*

Zevon is finished howling, and now he's gone all tenderhearted on us; never thought he'd be so lonely, eh? I should cool it. Melancholia threatens.

What am I doing here that's different from back home, or at school, or anywhere? I'm getting high and eating cereal and staring at the fucking wall. I feel the big empty that I sometimes get. Some people probably call it boredom, but for me it seems different, more profound. Pot is a mood enhancer, not necessarily a curative, and right now it's enhancing my bummer side.

I pop out the tape when the disco song starts. Going from the 'accidentally' song to the disco one is jarring. Don't you hate how they front load albums with the hits? I know I do. Not the Floyd, though. They've got integrity, like, their records are little movies for the mind. That's the stuff —this is our new symphonic music, our new opera, these rock musicians. Pink Floyd should do something really ambitious, a big, thematic double album like The Who did with *Tommy* and *Quadrophenia.*

The small galley kitchen is pretty rough around the edges—we've been eating out a lot. Footlong dogs and fries are a favorite, stoner beach food of the first order. I must stop thinking about it—everything's closed now. Depressed first, and now raging munchies. I can't win.

Or can I?

Right as I'm putting the cereal bowl into the tiny, stained sink I hear footfalls on the wrought-iron steps, and the creak of the screen door: Jamie's come home after all.

She gives me a hug. "I was fucked up earlier."

"I could tell."

"Guy traded me a couple black beauties for a dime. I mean, I done 'em before. But these jumping beans—yikes."

"You could've saved one for me." I don't really want it—like I said, never liked speed much. That's why I think acid was a bummer for me too, all that speedy crap that goes around. I doubt I've ever done any real good acid; at least that's what I think. Rather not take the chance though, with that or speed or coke or anything too heavy. I mean, I'm not some square or anything, but you can get fucked over on stuff if you're not careful, which is why I gave up most all of it. My point in asking her about sharing is my way of wondering why she wasn't thinking of me while she was off with those guys.

"I was bored," she said. "Waiting on your ass."

"I could tell."

"Don't start thinking we're together-together. Me hanging around."

I do worry about these feelings I'm cultivating for her. "We're just hanging out. Aren't we?"

"That's what I'm doing."

I proceed to describe to her in as precise a manner as possible how I perceive what's going on, concluding by re-stating my commitment to no commitment, in spite of the nascent feelings I have for her (which I downplay): "I'm really into you right now," I say, meaning very much the double entendre. "And that's a cool place to be. Doesn't mean anything. Just fun."

"Cool, huh? I thought it was hot in there."

"Oh, it is."

After that it doesn't take us long to get going. Before you know it, she's getting off like crazy. I guess it's the speed. I'm really shoving it in there, and the old bed frame is creaking and groaning under the strain. The Trojan feels tight, and a little dry on the inside, a touch uncomfortable.

I pull out and she flips over onto her hands and knees. She reaches back and pulls her cheeks apart as I slide back in. Within seconds, we're both raging again. The condom hurts a little, but I keep going.

A popping sensation, and my cock floods with slick sensation—the rubber has broken. "Oh, shit."

"Don't stop, don't *stop*—keep on."

So I do, and we both come like crazy, me pulling it out at the last possible freaking second and exploding all over her back.

Groaning, she keeps her butt sticking up in the air; I rest my still-rigid buddy in her crack, the remains of the condom tight around the base. "Um—whoa."

"We do pretty good together."

"It appears we do, Ray-Ray. Oh yeah."

●

AN AFTERNOON AT THE BEACH. Much time during the week, and little to do. Hedonistic pleasures abound. I begin almost immediately to stagnate, resisting the urge to wonder what's going on back in Columbia.

Laying around. Reading a paperback I found at the Olympic when we got breakfast earlier. *Man's Search for Meaning*. A philosophical overview by this cat named Victor Frankl, who got real, real deep while stuck in a concentration camp. I become consumed with the notion that the book was left there for me.

After only a few pages, though, I lay it down upon the loose yellow sand, which drifts across the cover. My own problems compared to those of the author—trying to make sense of the Holocaust, for god's sake—makes me seem like a dumb kid who doesn't know how good he has it. Frankl was caged like an animal, watching his fellow man gassed, burned, savaged. Me? Trapped by a life of privilege. *Hah*. Sometimes I disgust myself.

Jamie wanders over to a fantastically bored Duffy, who's sitting in his lifeguard's chair taking in the sleepy beachscape. Not many people around. Good. Easier to have a quick smoke that way. Duffy declined earlier when we offered; said he gave it up a while back after getting busted by the MBPD. It was only possession, but still. His folks made all sorts of threats. No way for them to know now, I told him, unless he gets caught red-handed. Not like there's a test for the shit like they do with your breath and motor skills during a DUI stop.

Grass. What was it like before the 1960's? Did anyone smoke at all? Apparently they did—in doing some reading in the Southeastern library one afternoon when I was supposed to be studying Modern American Lit, I came across some really hysterical stuff about the dangers of priapic negro jazz musicians and layabout Mexicans undermining the moral and social fabric of the nation: On dope, the blacks would go into a drug-frenzy and rape all the white women; the Mexicans simply wouldn't do the work we required of them as guests in our fair land. This was from the 1930's and thereafter—actual congressional testimony, no less.

Then I read this article from the fifties about *marihuana*, as it was spelled by that author, how it makes young people passive, and how the plant may in fact be a Communist plot to undermine our nation's ability and willingness to fight the insidious hordes massing on the other side of the ocean: The twentieth century version of Gog and Magog. So one minute pot makes you all crazy and the next lazy. Huh. And in my naiveté, I just thought it made you high.

Already the 60's seem like a century ago, but not as far back as, say, the world of *Happy Days* and *Laverne & Shirley* does to me. Everything from before my first levels of true awareness, maybe ten years ago, just at preadolescence, doesn't seem real, any more real than a cartoon or some old black and white movie.

I remember sitting with my grandfather when he was dying, watching wrestling on a tiny black and white set: The masked Super Destroyer versus Blackjack Mulligan; good old redneck Dusty Rhodes against the Nature Boy, Ric Flair. Granddad, he said he'd never get a color set. Said he didn't like it. Said, this was what he was used to, and he intended on it staying that way. He knew he was dying, but didn't talk about it. I know he knew because you could see it in his eyes when he thought no one was looking at him. He looked scared, which is not something I'd ever seen in his eyes—though the stories he told me about WWII led me to believe he was plenty scared back then, what with all those Jerries shooting at him.

Heart's beating hard inside my chest. Paranoid, thinking about death. Not something a young man like me should be too awfully concerned with, I know. But pot does that to you sometimes. Makes you consider the big picture, unlike booze, which just makes you all happy and silly. Pot is perfect for philosophical rumination. Gives you a sense of well being, mostly, and a sense of presence. Whenever I get drunk, I feel like a different person, not-me, like the little *Family Circus* ghost who causes all the accidents and mishaps. High, I am all there, right there, right now—sometimes too much.

I shake it off and my heart settles down. Questions abound, though, about the purpose of all this. Indolence is not necessarily my natural state, although there is something to be said for being a beach bum with no responsibility other than putting the next meal in my gut and keeping the rent paid, lest I end up like my vet friend from the first night. Already the memory of him, reeking of booze and drifting around downtown Myrtle Beach in the middle of a cold night, is less exotic than downright pitiable.

This is what my grandfather risked his life for, fighting somewhere across the sea, so I can lay about on the shore and ponder this facile foolishness? I wonder.

I miss him.

Alone.

I feel isolated again. I feel out of place and out of time. I don't belong to the hippy generation, which is fading away as fast as it arose—faster, even?—and I don't know what is going through people's minds anymore about anything. Like Carter says, we as a people seem to be in a funk. But maybe, just maybe, I'm projecting my own malaise onto the rest of the good folks of this great nation. Still, I ask, who are we, other than people who hate the brown-skinned towel heads who jack around with the price of our gasoline? Pete Townshend's new rock anthem seems hyper-appropriate. *Who are you. Who are you.* I know it is me about whom I ask this desperate, searching question. But I wonder if it isn't only me, rather, it is all of us who need ask of the true nature of the shared, collective identity we hold as Americans.

But then Jamie's back, and she yawns and stretches in the bright noon sunlight. "I love just laying around like this," she purrs. "I could do it forever."

"Me too." A lie. "Forever."

●

ENDLESS WALKS and meals of junk food. The waves lap gentle and inexorable against the shell-littered shore; otherwise, nothing much seems to happen.

Duffy sits in his life guard's chair and flips through comic books, drowsy and bored except when his supervisor comes rumbling by in a beat-up white Ford truck with *Beach Patrol* stenciled on the doors. The weather grows gradually warmer, though not by much.

Jamie and I play skee-ball and air hockey at the Electric Circus arcade, or else the Fun Plaza across the street. We sit at Marvin's drinking draft beer and watching clouds march across the azure sky. I take up smoking cigarettes again for half a day, then think better of it. I'm smoking so much grass I spit up brown lungers every morning as it is.

It is with shameless abandon Jamie flirts with any number of guys, thinking I don't notice. This is all well and good, you see, for what hold do I have over her? Does my moaning and thrusting into her admittedly-willing body give me some sort of de facto ownership? I think not: That is the way of the old world. Women, now, are their own beings.

Still—I feel protective of her, the chivalrous nature of my Southern upbringing coming through in my desire to shield her from the nefarious intentions of the blackguards and miscreants with whom her life story, sketchy as it is, appears to have been suffused, seemingly almost from the moment of her conception.

Jamie and I have little in common, I have discovered; not only are our histories as different as the vanilla and chocolate swirls of soft-serve we eat pretty much every day, but I've found our taste in many, many aspects of life ill-compatible. I dumb it down for her sometimes. Just makes it easier that way.

She hates that Zevon record, for instance, even though I wave the *Rolling Stone* magazine review at her, which says that, with this record, he has emerged as one of the most important new artists of the decade, right up there with Springsteen and Neil Young. I'm not much of a Springsteen fan, but Jamie, being a Jersey girl, most certainly is. She scoffs at the comparison between the two musicians.

"He's singin' about raping and killing a girl," she says of Zevon. "That's sick."

True enough. I'm unsure of what the songwriter's true intention is with such a tune—some kind of metaphor?—so I shrug and let it go.

I try again and again to draw her out, to find out who she really is, especially in those moments after we've made love. I feel odd at times to be so physically intimate with someone—repeatedly, vigorously—and yet feel as a stranger. With Sheila, she had been completely open to me that whole week leading up to our explosive night together, and if I felt as though I was getting away with something, at least I knew the kind of person she more or less was—or seemed like, anyway.

Jamie, though: I sometimes wonder if she's a little taleteller. Like, I don't even know that her name is Janet Leigh Allendale, not really. She could have been telling a fib, just wanting me to think that she was named after a famous movie actress.

Still—one night after a couple of beers and a fat doobie, her eyes are darker than normal, and her face is slack and seemingly off-guard, for once. Most of the time she's got a look on her cute mug like she's doing math equations in her head, biting her lip, with that little frown in between her almost-bushy, un-plucked brown eyebrows, a line that usually only completely disappears when she's coming.

"My mom, she ain't too bright, you know? Like, after my dad split, she didn't make much effort to find nobody better."

"I don't think that some people have a choice. Hard finding the right person." I stroke her leg, sitting next to her on the couch as "Sister Golden Hair" plays on the boombox courtesy of WKZQ. "Some people, they get trapped by their circumstances and don't know how to get out."

"Yeah, I guess. But see, my pop run off—he met some whore named Sally, a B-girl, my mom calls her, and then he was gone." She looks down. "But I was glad, you know? He—I mean, he didn't, he would—when we were alone in the house—?" Her voice has gotten so small that I can barely hear her. "Ya know."

I pull her close but her body remains stiff, arms folded tight across her stomach. "What did he do?"

Her lips pursed and chin all wrinkled like she just sucked a lemon, she's suffered an outbreak of patchy acne on her cheeks in the last few days; she says it happens right around her time of the month. All week she's been a foul mood too. I guess that all goes hand in hand—Nola-Marie used to be the same way. It doesn't bother me. Adds to her character; suits her, somehow. "Nothing I feel like talking about."

Something did go down—perhaps something horrible—but I don't push it. "Well, he ain't here now. Just you and me. I won't let anything happen to you."

She seems to snap out of it, finally. Jamie gives me a small, sad smile and flicks at an errant tear in the corner of her eye. "Oh yeah? Nobody been able to do that yet."

"I'm not like the rest of those scalawags. What you see is what you get."

"Is that so."

"I'm a gentleman of genteel Southern breeding, my dear," sounding like Foghorn Leghorn.

"I never known anyone but liars and cheats. Even Lars. I thought he was different. But you see what he done." She looks a tad wistful at the mention of her erstwhile lover's name, which annoys me. Who's here for her now? Him, or me?

In my own voice: "He's got his head up his ass. Anyone that would leave you, well, I'm not too confident of his smarts, ya know?" I kiss her on the top of the head. "Maybe it was meant to happen like that."

"Ain't nothing meant to happen."

"No?" I disagree only out of the desire to have a philosophical conversation for once. I'm pleased. There's plenty I don't believe in, but predestination is one of the biggies. "No underlying meaning?"

"It all just happens. You look at them church bastards: They'll say one thing, some say something else, and none of them live by it, hardly."

"Yeah, they'll say one thing to your face, then do quite the opposite when they think nobody's looking."

"I thought God was always looking."

I shrug and go back to the question at hand: "It's either all pre-determined, or else God has got His mighty finger on the scale, or else it's all up to us to figure out the right thing to do out of free will, or whatever. It's all a bunch of malarkey, if you ask me."

"Sounds like you spent some time working on this stuff."

"I spent the last two years at a major university."

"Okay, professor."

But I sound more sure than I am. Hard for me to believe in something that isn't there, though—or at least that you can't see. Hard for me to conjure faith because someone else tells me that's what is real. Empirical evidence, now, that's where it's at.

"What about Jesus, though? He gave everything up for us. You think none of it's true?"

I recall a conversation Chris and I had one night. "I think it was the greatest scam in history, like, ever," I quote my roommate, "that this one guy has been made out to be the true superman—the Son of God? C'mon. The resurrection is the biggest non-event that ever was. Don't see the difference between that and Peter Parker getting bitten by a fucking radioactive spider and then being able to walk up walls."

"So you don't think he was real?"

"I think there was an actual guy, sure. I think Christ was probably more in tune with his environment, with the nature of things, than a lot of folks were at the time. That would have made anyone seem pretty smart, wouldn't it? But the rest of the story, as Paul Harvey says on the radio, is kind of specious—the supernatural stuff. People wrote all that down afterwards. Doesn't mean it happened."

I start to tell her about Chris's theory that Flavius Josephus just made up the whole thing, but I don't want to lose her. She is engaged, looking into my eyes as though I've got some sort of answer to a question she's had for a long time. It makes me nervous; I feel as a fraud. But I go on: "You ever seen anyone come back from the dead?"

Bitter laughter. "My little brother died when he was just two. Did I tell you that?"

"No." How awful. "What happened to him?"

She doesn't elaborate much beyond the assertion that he got sick one winter, and her father kept putting off taking him in, saying it was just a cold, and how he couldn't afford no damn doctor. "By the time we went to the hospital—I was six—it was too late. The called it galloping pneumonia.”

“That's terrible.”

“My mom—that's all she talked about, you know, for like months afterwards? I could hear her in her bedroom, drunk, praying and praying and praying. 'Please let my little one come back, Jesus. *Please.*' It was real scary. That was right before Pops left. She didn't get better for a long time afterwards. She just kept drinking. Started bringing weirdos home. Some of them were just like Pops.” Jamie shudders and pulls away from me again.

I feel like an idiot. I'm supposed to protect this poor girl from not only the big, awful world, but also from her viscerally horrid past? I don't even know how to change a tire on the Mustang. I don't know from tragedy. The only loss I've known is that of old people dying off—which is what they're supposed to do, for pity's sake. I'm useless. “I wish I could make it all go away, sweetie.” The words sound thin, empty, inadequate.

“Aw, let's talk about something else. Let's go for a walk. Let's do something, Ray. The walls are closing in on me.”

And so we do; the wind on her face seems to blow away all those appalling memories of which she spoke, and then before you know it, there is the same old Jamie again, fun and happy and reasonably carefree.

•

THE FUN DOESN'T LAST. I point out a few days later—there is much idle time during which my mind does its usual scattershot gymnastics of reason and logic—that she could get a job too, after which we'd have even more money without worrying about selling grass. There isn't that much left anyway.

“I ain't getting a job. Forget it.”

“Well, hell, Jamie, just for the summer. And then—”

“You think I came to the beach to work? I'm here to party, bro.”

I try to explain how it would be a real help if she would at least take the time to buy some groceries, cook some food for me like a regular gal should, establish some sense of normalcy, of routine.

"You Southerners." It sounds like *suth-a-nahs*. "Bunch of mama's boys. Cook yer own food. Or get a negro maid like Beulah."

Sting. Ouch. The involuntary flush of recognition at an honest, though hurtful, commentary.

"I didn't mean it like that," I say in a flat tone, a little too like my own voice for comfort. "I just thought we were partners, you know."

Of course I'm also sick of all this crap around here, the sub sandwiches and hot dogs and pizza and milkshakes—what are we, kids? I want a decent meal. I struggle against it, but have to admit the thought of my grandmother's Sunday dinner spread makes me swoon—fried chicken, potatoes with a thick and greasy pool of gravy, macaroni with sharp cheddar cheese, squash with onions cooked down until the vegetables are almost caramelized, hand-snapped pole beans with a chunk of fatback plopped in the middle, collard greens with hot pepper vinegar, creamed white summer corn, banana pudding, lemon meringue pies, blackberry cobbler, homemade peach ice cream from granddad's old metal churn.

A vision: The old man—my old man, not granddad—grunting and futzing with the ancient churn, spilling rock salt, cranking, cranking, cranking the handle, all of us swatting flies and waiting with baited impatience for the cream to form. "Everybody keep they pantyhose on," he'd always say. "Cream's a coming."

My stomach grumbles like a bear coaxed out of its hibernation too early.

"I'm here to have a good time, all the time," Jamie says, petulant and whiny. "I ain't nobody's nursemaid. Not for Lars, and sure as shit not for you, Ray-Ray."

As though she's deprived, somehow, in our day-to-day life of getting high and screwing and generally dicking around! What inappropriate, insulting insolence! But I don't tell her that. When she gets like this, I've discovered there's just nothing for it.

I sigh in defeat. "So, what, you want a pizza? Or another sub sandwich? Peaches is still open, I think…"

"I DON'T BELIEVE YOU. You turkey. You have *got* to be kidding," Chris says when told of my new career. "You must be out of your mind."

"Not at all, my good man. Isn't this what I wanted? A complete change? A one-eighty in the opposite direction?"

"I think you're full of shit, cuz. C'mon."

I'm on a payphone checking in with my old roomie, mainly to make sure he's got someone to sublet from me for—well, for an indefinite period. I'm watching the light traffic cruising by the strip on a sunny Friday afternoon. I'm on my way to work, looking forward to a decent evening of dry-panted taunting, though I know I'll get dunked early tonight, even if I don't want to admit it to myself.

"I say, old boy, it's quite the bit of fun with these hayseeds. You must give it a try one day."

"No thanks. The life of a carny is not exactly what I'm shooting for."

He goes on to relate a series of quasi-interesting anecdotes, most of which are about the weirdo guy he's got sub-leasing my bedroom for the summer, a kid he met in the music school who's heavily into punk, the Sex Pistols on back to the Stooges and all sorts of other harsh stuff. As a matter of fact, I can hear Johnny Rotten in the background during the phone call.

I immediately decide to begin working on a Cockney, blue-collar accent, an annoying, angry bloke with an imaginary safety pin through his lip, with the attitude to match. It'll be a scream. I'll probably end up soaking wet—but hopefully a financial success.

The conversation meanders on as I drop another dime into the phone. Traffic has picked up. I watch a young kid a few feet away, a blonde boy of about ten in a striped t-shirt, white shorts, and with a puka shell necklace around his skinny neck. He's waiting, rather impatiently, I might add, for enough of a break in the traffic to dart across. He's all jumpy, not in a druggy, speedy way, just in that little kid manner, one who's all pumped up about being at the beach. Or maybe he just needs to pee.

"So anyway," Chris drones on, "I nail this one chick finally, Nancy. She's a flautist with the student orchestra, right, and so I make this joke about Claude Bolling that she doesn't get and then—"

"HEY!" I drop the phone and run over, grabbing the kid at the last second. I have observed that he looked right one last time, just before a van turned onto the main drag from 4th Avenue, but he didn't look left. I make a dive and grab the kid from behind just as he makes his move off the curve. I barely catch him; we both tumble into the filthy gutter. The van's brakes squeal and the smell of tire-rubber drifts into my nostrils.

The kid is screaming. "Get offa me get offa me *MOM*—"

"Now, now, young man, you's almost run over just now. Show some gratitude." I admonish the impulsive youth who I have saved from a bleak future as roadkill.

The driver of the van, an old codger with crazy, wispy white hair framing a slack-jawed pie face, stares at us both as he slowly moves on ahead of the honking horns behind him.

"Let me go, you weirdo!" The kid scrambles to his feet and runs back into one of the motels.

I go back to the phone, but Chris has hung up. Inside my jeans, I can feel a flap of skin—my knee is scraped. The fucking little turd didn't have a mark on him, though. The sacrifices we make in the name of public safety. They should pin a medal on me.

6

NIGHTTIME IN THE SWITCHING YARD

I get around to talking to my mother again one boring afternoon. She begs and cajoles and tries to convince me to come home, or at least back to Columbia, and school, and real life, as she puts it. She tries lighthearted nonchalance, which then turns to anger and threats when I don't respond in the manner she'd obviously hoped.

"But son—what about Easter? You c'ain't tell me you're willing to miss my Easter ham."

"Nope. Not coming home, like I said. Not even for that. I mean—y'all didn't even start going back to church until Daddy decided to run for Lonny Sheehan's seat. *Screw* Easter." It comes out more far more mean-spirited than necessary. My mother hasn't done anything to me, not really. The idea of driving back and sitting down for Easter Sunday dinner, even though the lure of the meal is appealing, makes me feel six years old.

"Oh, Ray-Ray." She trails off, boo-hooing.

However I feel about my mother's culpability with regard to what ails me, this is all oh-so tiresome, and I hang up on her. This payphone deal is great—they can't call you back and start up again. Having the last word. Now if that isn't the sweetest, I don't know what is.

But last word or otherwise, there remains a knot in my stomach for a long time afterwards, a sensation I don't understand, a mix of irritation and regret and bewilderment—the big three emotions that have characterized this phase of my life. Familiar, these feelings, but friends they are not.

●

"BUT MAMA—*PLEASE*." The kid is pre-pubescent, chubby, with Coke-bottle glasses and a flat-top like Sgt. Carter from *Gomer Pyle*. His dad and mom both have similar ocular devices propped on their flat noses, along with the same dumpy physicality, pale skin, and rounded stoop-shoulders: they are truly one of those families who all look exactly alike.

"You can't hit that thing son! Now come on. You said you wanted to ride rides, not play no damn games. That's all you done all afternoon."

"But we have to go home tomorrow. *Please*."

Bogart: "If the little man thinks he's got a shot at me, lady, then you should let him take it."

"You're getting wet, mister."

"You think you can take me out, slugger? Fat chance." I don't sound all that funny—just kind of threatening. An off-night for me thus far, my first. Wind's cold coming off the ocean, the Pavilion is lightly attended, my buzz is long gone and I'm losing interest in the whole routine. *Already!* Even Maybelle sits staring at me, wondering where the spark is. She's not alone.

"I said no and I meant no, Jason, now—"

"But Daddy said I was gonna get to play baseball and that I oughta practice and that maybe I could even play first base and—"

The argument goes on, the father looking back and forth from mother to son with an expression of bafflement and placation: He can go either way, whatever will get him onto the next problem, the next argument. The boy looks up at him, imploring, hopeful, and his daddy shrugs, mumbling something I can't hear.

Mama acquiesces, digging in her huge, white purse. "*Here*." She gives the youth a few crumpled bills. "Hurry up and get this over with."

Game show host: "That's right ladies and germs, the young man with the pitching arm is about to take his best shot, and go for the big prize of seeing our hero, Buzzno the Clown, get his wrinkled bottom damp. Step right up, little Johnny Too-Bad, and," I now go into a more sinister, Scottish burr, like an evil James Bond, "take your best shot laddie. Take it like a man. If you think you can." The smell of hot, fresh caramel corn wafts over me, and my stomach growls.

The kid steps up to the duct-tape line with his three gray baseballs. He carefully puts two of them at his feet, and looks not at me, but at the target. His face is pink and his eyes huge. He's licking his lips. A few other patrons sidle up, including a couple of teenagers with long, stringy hair and open-mouthed expressions of either vapidity or utter tedium on their pale, pock-mocked faces.

"I hate that fucken clown," one of them says. "Dunk his ass."

An old man in plaid shorts passing by at that moment removes the toothpick on which he'd been sucking and shakes it at the youth: "You young'uns watch your mouth. This here's a family park."

"Let's see what you got, kid," Bogart says from somewhere inside my throat. I feel detached, going through the motions, repeating voices within the same routine.

The little boy, probably about eleven, fingers the first ball, licks his lips, then draws back and lets fly… and the baseball doesn't even make it all the way to the front of the booth, bouncing once and rolling to a stop at the bottom of the netting.

"Oh shoot, oh shoot," he says in humiliation as the teenagers snicker and his mother rolls her eyes.

"I told you, Jason. Hurry up, now."

"Take your time, son," his meek dad offers. "Keep your eye on the target." Mama shoots the beleaguered head of the household a withering look and he recants: "I mean, c'mon now."

"God-dog, beau." Mean Redneck hectors the boy from inside the safety of my wire cage. "You ain't gonna make it in the big leagues like 'at. Wind that arm up and gimme somepin' I can work with." I scratch under the fright wig and adjust the sunglasses. I stifle a yawn. " C'mon now, son."

He picks up another ball. "Okay okay okay," he says to himself. He leans back and lets fly like a shot-putter, stumbling forward with the force of his effort. The battered, scarred baseball goes wild, striking the cage right in front of my face. "Whoa, Nelly. We got us a wild one tonight."

The kid is further agitated and rubicund of cheek. He snatches up the last ball from in between his wide, flip-flopped feet, his face a mask of determination. He looks back at his dad, who shrugs—it appears to be the man's only form of expression—and the boy peers at me with a beseeching sort of hope, as though I can make it happen for him, which of course I can't. Well, I could, I suppose—but I ain't. This is a good character building exercise for the little tyke.

Game Show Host: "One last chance to hit the target ladies and germs, and take home the big prize—your choice of a lovely living room suite by Lay-Z-Boy, or else a trip to French *GUIANA*, and an all expenses paid stay at *bee-you-tee-ful* Devil's Island. Or else," I intone, "merely pride in a job well done, perhaps. Let go," I conclude in a reasonable Alec Guinness. "Trust your feelings, Luke."

His eyes go wide at the *Star Wars* reference. He grins at me, nods. With a grunt, he fires off what is a Hail Mary of a toss.

The crowd holds its collective breath, as do I. The ball spins in a great arc, up, up, and then down toward... the target! But, having lost most of its forward momentum, the ball merely grazes the reinforced bullseye and drops to the ground.

I make the game-show buzzer sound—the one of failure, of the incorrect answer, of the missed chance for glory—and the kid looks stricken, in disbelief that he *hit the target* but that it didn't cause me to fall into the water.

And then he goes absolutely ape-shit. "But I hit it! But I hit it! It's not fair! He cheated. He *cheated!*" He starts to cry uncontrollably, as though he's being beaten. "*Nooooo!*" he screams as he mother drags him away. "I got to try *again!*"

His father walks past and gives me his patented, befuddled shrug, and I feel awkward about the appalling display of disappointment on the part of the chubby kid. But he took his chance, and if he failed, at least he tried. That's what I would tell him if he were my son.

I try to goad the teenagers into taking a shot at me, and then some other folks coming and going into the Pavilion, but I can't seem to fish them in tonight. The shift drags on until I finally get dunked a couple of times, but that only makes me angry. I keep hearing my mother's voice, saying things like: *Son, what are you doing still at the beach?*

HOME ON A WEEKNIGHT, nothing going on but the steady breeze off the water and moths flitting about the yellow bug-light outside the screen door. Somewhere inland, a train rumbles through. Listen to the whistle cry. It's a sound I associate with late nights lying in my childhood bed, imagining hopping aboard one of those freight cars, as though people still did it like hoboes back in my grandfather's day. People were desperate, then; they weren't riding the rails for some cheap, romantic thrill.

Even more worrisome is the nagging sensation, after I notice the sound of the mournful, howling engine somewhere inland, wafting over to me in the lilac dusk, that the train whistle has inspired the same longing for change, for adventure, of which I'd dreamt in my narrow boy's bed. But wasn't I living out the fantasy? Hadn't I left my life (as I understood it) completely behind for this bohemian, free-from-responsibility, hardscrabble, blue-collar, honest-living career as a carny? With my experience, I could even join an actual traveling fair or carnival, and really see the sights that the country has to offer, now couldn't I?

I remember well the fairs that would come through Tillman Falls each autumn and spring, the barkers and the colored balloons all set up in the big field next to the IGA. I recall watching my father get taken by a grizzled operator, a huge black man with an ugly mole hanging off his lip, and a jaunty, purple beret cocked to the side on his substantial head. He'd assured Dad that, if he took just one more chance on the game (whatever it was), he would make back all that he had lost, and then some. Dick DeKalb left with an empty wallet and a red face; a smart guy like him should have known better. He'd had a few that night, though. His judgment in the evening is rarely as sound as it is in the light of the morning.

Jamie, pensive and annoyed, sits alongside me. She wants to get into some fun, but I have been noncommittal all evening. She's smoking a clove and biting her nails. She's on speed again. I don't know where and how she gets it, but she does. We don't spend every minute together, you know.

"C'mon, Ray. I wanna go out tonight," she says once more.

"A bit tired, maybe. Thought about going to a movie."

"*Feh.* I feel like dancing." Her knees bouncing up and down make it seem as though she's already started.

I hem and haw a bit, but she finally insults me into acquiescing, and I agree to hit the streets. After all, what else is there to do?

○

THE DANCE FLOOR at Mother Fletcher's is not too crowded on this weeknight in April—mostly townies. I didn't think underage high school kids could get in here, but that's mostly what it seems like. Jamie and I have been inside for a while, drinking beer and dancing.

I've been here at the beach a whole month, now, almost. Seems longer. I try to think of what I've learned from the experience thus far, but my mind is a stoned, fuzzy blank.

The strings, mellophone and choir on the huge speakers herald the fifty-thousandth spin of Yvonne Elliman's *Saturday Night Fever* tune. Jamie pulls me out on to the floor and we spin slowly around. *"If I can't have you, I don't want nobody bay-BEE..."* The space between our bodies is negligible, warm, increasingly damp. Her small breasts are flat against my own bony chest. She's looking up at me with a goofy, stoned smile. Her eyes droop. We really toked up before coming over here, which calmed her down. The flashing lights and loud music are a little too enhanced, almost a bit much for me. Not for Jamie though. She cut a rug earlier to Pablo Cruise, dancing around until a light sheen of sweat covered her body.

"Oh, *shit*." Her eyes no longer droop, and she sucks in her breath as though she's been punched. She pushes away from me with another small curse. "Paco—oh, *no*."

"What the hell—!" I feel a hand on my shoulder, hard, a fucking Vulcan nerve pinch.

"That's my girl, you little prick."

I do not turn voluntarily; I am in fact spun around to face my accuser. And thus is my introduction to Paco Veracruz. Jamie has mentioned him here and there, what a hard-case streetwise dude he is; what a dangerous little gangster he can be. Pablo Cruise, Paco Veracruz. The names dance around in my mind together.

"Paco, don't hurt him."

"And why shouldn't I?" Paco's big, Latino, not a hippy at all, a real grease-ball, in my not-so-humble opinion.

"I don't even know him—I just met him tonight!"

"Tonight, eh?"

He's glaring right through me, smiling, a thin mustache above his lip that I notice hides—barely—a small, jagged scar. "You sure seem like you know her, *ese*, putting your hands on her like that. I should kick your fucken *ass*."

His accent is part Hispanic, part dumb northeast guy. He's Mexican, or something, by way of Jersey. I'm just guessing, though. Whatever he is, I'm not afraid of him.

Okay, I'm afraid. "Nah, nah, man." My own Southern accent stands out in stark relief to his own. "I didn't know her before just now, beau. Seriously now." I try to play it dumb and hayseed. Why I'm more worried about getting punched instead of defending Jamie's honor against this coarse, crude interloper is anyone's guess. Maybe because at heart I'm a pussy.

"Bullshit. You know how long I been in this stink-ass club, watching *y'all*," he drawls with a sour expression on his face. "A long-ass time."

Ass, ass, ass, I want to say, *is that all you think about, Paco?* I consider one of my little funny accents. The outrageous French of the castle guards in *Holy Grail*? A mocking Brooklynese of my own? *Tank you veddy much*? The new one, the cockney punk rocker?

"Well, look here," I finally shout as Yvonne Elliman fades into K. C. and his wee bit o' Sunshine Band. "I reckon I'd be mad too. But, she ain't said word-one about no Paco, bro. I—I got my own girl back home anyway."

Jamie flashes me an arched eyebrow—*oh, really?*

"Well, you should get your ass back home to her, *ese*. You know what I mean?" Paco flashes open his leather jacket, and there's the fucking butt of a revolver—a goddamn shoulder holster like Dirty Harry or Bullit any of a million TV and movie cops. "You the one who stole her from Lars?"

"Nah—I mean, who?" Lars—another real winner now best forgotten. I look forward to the moment when I can forget this motherfucker too.

"You should send his mama a sympathy card. She's prolly in the waiting room at Mercy Hospital, huh? You know—see, he stole her from me first—right, *Jaime*?" he asks.

"Don't flatter yourself."

He pulls her close to him; she doesn't resist. "And now I got you to deal with, redneck boy. You like dis redneck boy, *Jaime?* Tell truth."

She looks at me with wide eyes. "I done told you I don't know him, Paco. I was just dancing and he—"

"Shut up, *bitch.*"

Jamie pushes away from Paco. He laughs at what must be a stricken, pale expression on my face. In that instant, I feel again as a child, that chubby sixth grader who wouldn't lose his baby fat for another few years. All of the maturity I've been pretending to feel over the past few weeks (except on the occasion of those excruciating phone calls with family members) melts away like a snow cone in a toddler's hand at high noon on the asphalt of the Pavilion. No funny voices come to mind; no voice at all, as a matter of fact.

"Let's split from outta this fucking rank-ass redneck disco," Paco says, pleasant and cheerful. "Since neither of us seem to know you, let's go get ourselves acquainted, Southern boy."

And so he leads us both out of Mother Fletcher's and into the cool spring night.

I'm full of rage, but also paralyzed with fear. I do nothing but shuffle along in the sand off to the side of my girlfriend and her dangerous ex, as I now think of him. I am one step to the left and a pace behind the two of them, as though I am some lesser officer trailing behind his boss, a conquering general of power and *gravitas.* Paco shoots me a look over his leather-jacketed shoulder every now and then, sometimes hard and mean, sometimes giving me a sly wink. Little puffs of smoke from the Swisher Sweet tucked into the corner of his cruel mouth loft into the chilly ocean breeze. Neither the winks nor the smoke reassures me about this predicament.

"Smell that ocean." His nostrils flare; he coughs a bit on the exhalation. "All salty and shit. Like your pussy, babe." He pulls Jamie close to him.

"Quit it, Paco. Just quit it, now." She tries to pull away from him as we walk along the beach with the boardwalk above us, a few vacationers and townie kids shuffling along but otherwise deserted. I'm terrified even more with each passing moment; there are so few people around that, should he decide to, Paco could get away with quite a bit—especially underneath the 14th Avenue pier rapidly approaching.

The waves break along the pilings as we go under the wooden structure, where Paco stops and holds up a fist like a soldier on point who has detected suspicious activity up ahead.

"You see dat shit?" He leans up against a piling, the brown, damp wood smelling of the ocean that laps up against it with the coming and going of the moon. He pulls Jamie close to him; she is stiff, hugging herself as though cold.

"Who, me?"

His eyes are flinty in the dim light. He gestures with the smoldering cigar toward the ocean. "Turn around and look down there, redneck boy."

My insides quivering, I gaze down the length of the pier's underside, the pilings closer and closer together, brownish foam rolling in among them with each small wave. The criss-cross pattern of the support beams looks like elaborate monkey bars leading outward into the gray turbidity of the unforgiving ocean, offering danger far beyond that of any playground. "What am I looking for?"

"That's like a tunnel, yeah? Looks like a tunnel going off into the ocean." He laughs and looks down at Jamie, who's chewing her lip in fear. "Where it lead, though? Where it lead to?"

"The continental shelf?" I mutter.

"Shelf, like in the pantry, or something? Naw, naw. A tunnel don't lead to no shelf."

If I know Jamie—and I'm wondering now just how well I in fact do— she's thinking of some plan, some way to escape. From both of us, probably. Look at me. What am I doing to stand up to this guy? *Alla da sudden Mistah Motahmouth can barely put two words together* I think in Jamie's Jersey patois.

"Okay—how is it like a tunnel?"

Paco gets this contemplative look on his face. "My nena—my granny, like you rednecks would say—she died, all right? Yeah. She died, but you know what? They brought her back. Thump-thump with those paddle-things, and then…? She come back, little man. And you know what she told me? Once she woke up again?"

I shrug and fold my arms across my chest, the first gesture I make even remotely in the ballpark of nonchalance, or even perhaps defiance if seen with the right eyes.

"She say she went down this tunnel, yeah? And God was there. Or Jesus, or whoever, yeah?"

"Heard that one too. A bright light."

"Okay, okay, good. Now, you want to know how that tunnel is like this one here?"

There is cold fire in my belly now—but not the icy fury of combat readiness, only of abject terror. I don't read minds—but I know what he's going to say. "*Nuh*-no."

"That tunnel's the last thing you gonna see before you go down the other tunnel, see?" He has the gun in his hand.

"For god sakes," my voice breaks. "Why? What did I do?"

"For fucking my lady. That's why."

"I never fucked her," I scream out. "Not once."

"He didn't, Paco, he didn't." Her accent now sounds more like his, more Latino. *Didn't* sounds like *didden*.

"You sure about that?"

Jamie and I exchange a furtive look. Something in her eyes is hard now, annoyed even. What an encumbrance I've become to her—just like Lars, I guess, and Paco before him. "Fuck you both," she yells out, pushing away and running north on the beach, her feet sliding every which way in the loose sand.

Paco laughs at her retreating back. "Damn. *Como alma que lleva el Diablo.*"

My Spanish is for shit, but I know that Diablo is the devil. And in this moment I feel as though the dark one is indeed standing before my eyes.

"And I thought we were doing so well with her." I feel as though I'm going to faint, the words of my lame attempt at humor sounding hollow and far away.

Paco, ever the cool customer, puts the gun away. Still chuckling, he says, "Homeboy, you think I care 'bout that little cooze?"

"Sure seems like it, pal."

"Nah. I don't care what she did do, what she *didden* do, none of that shit. Jamie, it ain't like she—well. You know what kinda girl she is by now, I *reckon*."

"She seemed nice enough. At first."

He gives me a knowing nod, accompanied by a pitying little crease of a frown between his dark eyes. "Now let's go have us a legitimate discussion. Like two men."

I resist the urge to ask him if I might first change my underwear, instead following him from under the pier toward Ocean Boulevard.

7

———

VERACRUZ

"Thing is with these women, *man*," Paco says, smacking loudly in between bites of a foot-long hot dog slathered with relish and onions and yellow mustard, "you c'ain't trust them far as you can throw them. Yeah?"

"Dude, I hear you." I can see Nola Marie's smiling face. "No doubt."

"It's why I ain't tied down to that chick. Or any girl."

With Jamie off somewhere, it's as though he's trying to put me at ease, connecting with me in the only way he can—through our mutual masculinity. It ain't workin'.

I wonder if I'm dreaming all this. Time seems elongated, like how people describe their perception in moments of high impact stress such as a car accident: All is in slow motion, every small movement, every bit of philosophical musing, each bite he takes of the hot dog. Now that I know there's a gun under his leather jacket, I can but stare at the small bulge produced by the weapon.

We're in Peaches Corner, my now-familiar diner that sits diagonally across the boulevard from the Pavilion. Peaches has been around forever —*Since 1936,* the sign out front informs—and is the restaurant that provides "family dining in air-conditioned comfort." The eatery stays open late for just this kind of traffic. There is sand—just a little—in every nook and cranny of this old place. The vinyl, round stools lined up against the cracked Formica counter look as though they've held a million sets of damp swim trunks; the waitress looks a hundred years older than she probably is. Paco told me to order whatever I wanted, but I've eaten here so much now that I don't really care for the food anymore.

"L'il bitch like her? My advice?"

"Go on."

"You best keep one eye on your wallet." He grunts and smacks and slurps at a cherry Coke through a straw. "If it was me."

I want to kick this guy. He's talking about Jamie, about *my girl*. But he holds all the cards. He's in charge—and he knows it. There's a part of me, though, that wonders how right he might be about her. After all—he must surely know this girl better than I do.

Jealousy roils in my gut as I wonder how well he's known her—how many times he has had her—and then I go hot all over. "She seems okay to me," I mumble. "She's had a rough time of it."

"Not that sob story. Shameless, she is."

I fight off the old racist urges from my upbringing, the sense of privilege, and of class. I should be in this subservient position, and to a spic, no less? *No, no*, I think in between bouts of terror. Don't be like that. He's just another thug, regardless of his ethnicity. He's a common street hoodlum. Wouldn't matter if he were green, or from Mars. Still be the same shitty situation. The color of the gunpowder in the bullet is all that matters.

"So how you meet Jamie, anyway?"

"She was staying in the same place as me at first. Said her boyfriend just ditched her, left her here. I felt like—I thought she needed a friend."

"Yeah, bro. She does. She definitely does. Girl ain't worth a damn on her own. She need somebody to steer her in the right direction. Otherwise, she go right off the rails. Just like with that dumb-shit Lars. He ain't a real Einstein, him."

"No? I only met him in passing."

"They both shoulda known it wouldn't work out."

Smoke from a long, thin menthol is curling up from the ashtray as the waitress sits behind the counter on her own stool, thumbing idly through a *People* magazine with Debby Boone and her dad on the cover. (Which reminds me that if I hear "You Light Up My Life" one more time I'm going to grab Paco's gun and finish myself off *for* him, you know?) The only other patrons besides my new friend and me are a young couple sharing a sundae at the other end of the counter, oblivious to all but each other's teenaged eyes, and a grizzled old beach bum at the opposite end with a camouflage ball cap tipped back on his wrinkled, leathery head. He's chuckling to himself, flipping through a newspaper and sipping coffee, offering an occasional muttered comment to some tidbit of the *Sun News*. His weathered skin looks as though the sun is indeed giving him some news: Stay indoors.

I consider laying one of the voices on Paco, to see if he'll be amused. "Yes, yes, the girl's quite a pip," I say in Upper Class Twit. "As you so astutely point out, perhaps she just needs direction."

Paco laughs, but mirthless. "That's what I'm sayin'. She need someone to rein her in, keep on the straight and narrow." He regards me evenly as he wipes mustard from his thin mustache. "She fuck you over quick as look at you."

"So you keep telling me."

A flicker of hurt—of humanity—in his deep, brown eyes; a melancholy tone. "Bro, I been there. That's all."

I suck on my own soda pop and it gurgles; the sound is a comforting one. My mother always stuck a Coke in front of me anytime I acted like I wanted one of their grownup drinks, which always looked so enticing to me (until at a cookout once when I finally tasted one of Daddy's mysterious and sharply spicy libations, and the whiskey turned my stomach). The sensation of carbonated bubbles breaking on the tip of my nose will most certainly remain a cherished memory into my golden years. Assuming, that is, I survive my encounter with Señor Veracruz—if that is his name in the first place.

In spite of my fear, I press on in Twit parlance. "Now see here, old boy —how might I extricate myself from this awkward and delicate situation?"

Paco frowns. "Why you talkin' like that all of a sudden?"

"Just what I do. What I do for a living, s'all."

"You got a job doin' funny voices?"

Saying so floods me with self consciousness. "Yeah. Somehow."

"What, you're like Steve Martin, or somebody?"

I blush at the comparison: I've all but memorized Martin's comedy albums. Instead of thanking Paco for such a meaningful compliment, I instead tell him about the gig at the Pavilion, about Pugliesi, the whole story.

He's bemused but dismissive. "Carny, eh? Scumbags. Carnies do a lotta dope though, huh?"

"Some, yeah. More of a family operation, I think." In truth, I have no idea. I haven't made many friends around the Pavilion. Most of the other workers regard me with suspicion, if not outright loathing. I can only imagine what they say about the college boy behind his back.

"You?"

"Me what?"

"Do a lotta dope, *man?*" He leans in all conspiratorial, and gives me one of his winks.

"Never touch it. Well—I mean. Ya know."

He has a look of skepticism, like *no-way, Jose.* "You rubes, you don't get around much. You don't party?"

I've had enough of these redneck insults. My heritage has nothing to do with my behavior. I'm not some small town, cornpone, tobacco-chewing nimrod. Well, the small town part, maybe. But, hell—I've been around. Sure I have. "Grass, yeah. Toke on some reefer, you know how it is. But who cares, it'll probably be legal before too much—"

My drink goes flying as he grabs me by the neck of my ringer T-shirt, his movement sudden and brutal as a cornered rattlesnake. "Grass? You like *grass,*" he once again says in a bad Southern impression, stretching and distorting the "a" sound. "You know who that *grass* belongs to, *jefe*? Do you?"

"It's—I didn't—it's not—I'm sorry." The only voice coming from me is constricted, a thin wheeze like an old man with a tube in his nose begging for absolution prior to death.

"Freddie? I mean, *jeez*—!" The waitress has slid off her stool and lumbered toward us, a painted face turned into a mask of weary annoyance.

Freddie, a sleepy eyed, diminutive fry cook with a nose like an aircraft warning beacon, hobbles out from the kitchen area looking as though he's been awakened from a peaceful nap. "What, what?"

Paco produces a fat roll of cash, though it mostly looks like small bills. "Naw, naw, people, we just messing around, my homeboy and me." He peels off a five-spot and drops it on the counter in the puddle left by my soft drink. "Yee-all keep da change, now, ya hear?"

"Get outta here, you punks. Season ain't even started yet. I ain't gonna put up with no horseplay." She stands with her arms folded and mumbles, "Not until bike week at least." Bike week, I understand, is an enormous motorcycle rally that draws beaucoup tourist dollars to Myrtle Beach right before Memorial Day weekend. Pugliesi has already told me to be wary about taunting the bikers. "You be careful. They'll pick up that cage and-a drop you into the ocean," he forewarned me last week when the subject came up.

"We don't make no trouble, pretty lady." Paco flashes a yellow-toothed grin at her. "My bro and me is on vacation."

I look him over for what seems like the first time: six-two, some speckles of dark acne scattered about, a big hook nose that makes him look more Middle Eastern than Latino. He's a real prize, this one, especially in the cold fluorescent light of the diner. Not a real handsome customer, this Paco. But money talks, and bullshit walks, as the patriarch of the DeKalb clan often reminds me, so it doesn't surprise me that Jamie would get mixed up with some guy like this. She's looking for someone to take care of her, I think. Someone with money and power and influence, none of which I currently possess in any quantity worthy of her desires.

Paco is right about one thing, that I don't know the real her at all, maybe. I don't know why I should let some gangster like Paco Veracruz change my mind about sweet little Jamie, though—I know him even less than her. I mean, he's a loose cannon, and a liar to boot: He acted like we were friends earlier. But now?

He propels me onto the sidewalk—gently enough, however, so as not to attract attention from the MBPD cruiser rolling past—and says, "All right, little man, now let's roll over and see where you and my old lady been shacking up. We got a lot to figure out."

"I had no idea about you. I'm not into stealing somebody's girl."

"You like Jamie, though. Right?"

I'm struck dumb. It seems no answer I give could be right. "I'm just trying to be her friend."

"Well, we gonna put you two 'friends' to work all summer long here in podunk, and I don't mean doing no dumb-ass voices. Now hot-foot it us over there before I get irritated with you slow-ass Southerners again."

WHEN WE GET to the apartment, Jamie's nowhere to be found—but there's no way to get around the fact that she lives there. Jamie-junk, as I have taken to calling her leavings, is everywhere: Panties, feminine products, hair scrunchies, other girly crap, including a couple pairs of her sandals. It's obvious that habitation with me occurs in this particular abode, and I can only hope that Paco has been truthful when he said that part didn't matter.

He picks up a pair of her undergarments from the back of the tattered armchair against the wall near the bed; he smells of them deeply, lasciviously. But then he grimaces and flings the threadbare, blue panties across the room. "Smells like *ass*."

"Jamie's not a real Betty Crocker when it comes to housekeeping."

"So you is shackin' up with her." A flat statement. "My old lady. And you."

"You got me." I feel the blood drain from my face. What are my choices? He's either going to kill me or not, no matter what I say or do. "I guess it's obvious."

"Nah, nah, bro." He busts a gut laughing and slips his jacket off. He's wearing a yellow t-shirt with a triumphant Pele wearing his soccer uniform and raising his fist in the air, the screen print fading and starting to flake off. "I'm just fucking with you. I ain't give a rip."

Paco plops down in the chair, adjusts the shoulder holster and pulls off his black, high-heeled disco boots. On the walk over, he retrieved a backpack from his ride, a tricked-out Trans-Am that screams pull-me-over. I wondered in that moment just how smart a drug dealer Paco truly was, driving around in that cop magnet.

He extracts a fifth of Jack Daniels and a joint from a plastic baggie of loose, green pot. The doober is bigger by half than the Swisher Sweet he'd been sucking on earlier.

"So what, you smoke all that other shit? The grass Jamie stole?" He breaks the tax-stamp seal on the bottle of Jack and takes a pull. He coughs at first as the liquor scalds his throat, then takes another pull. He then fires up the bomber with a flourish from a pink Bic lighter. "You know?"

"Jamie had some pot when we hooked up, right? How was I to know?" Zevon's voice interjects itself: *How was I to know, she was with the Russians too?* "How was I to know it was yours? Hell, I thought it was—well."

"You thought it was what?"

"I thought it was Lars' weed."

Paco's eyes are hard, cold steel again. "So you knew it was, like, stolen goods. But you smoked it anyway. You didn't care. You don't got no fucking sense of right and wrong, whiteboy. You know that?" Paco drinks more, bubbling the liquor. "That worries me. No wonder yee-all's getting along so good, youse and Jamie."

He puts the bottle down and fingers the butt of the gun sticking out of his stained armpit. The salt air wafts through a window; I think I hear the creaking of the iron stairs outside but make no move to investigate. I'm half hoping he'll offer me a pull on that liquor—I'm scared shitless yet again. From the high to the low for the rest of my life with this guy.

"Lemme tell you a few stories about Little Miss Muffett you been dancing with, *jefe*." Paco goes on to relate a profane and descriptive recent sexual history of Jamie, much of which I can believe owing to her skill level, but some of which almost sounds like sour grapes: Paco, at times, seems almost pained to describe these nasty tidbits about the girl for whom I'd previously allowed myself to believe I might be tumbling into deeper emotion. It's pathetic but true: I had to stop myself from telling her *I love you I love you I love you* the last time we fucked. Hell, I felt that way about Nola-Marie the first time she let me stick it in there too. I feel shallow, suddenly.

"Well, it ain't like I was planning to marry her," I offer. "But thanks for the history lesson."

"*De nada.*" He looks at me all sad and offers the bottle. "You want a pull on this?"

"Yeah. Sure." I take it from him and the smell of the brown liquor immediately reminds me of home. "I really came here to get away from drama, man. Never intended to step on anyone's weed, or girlfriends either, for that matter."

"That's a beautiful thing you're saying. Now, let me tell you how you're gonna make it up to me. Make some money that you need, and that I need, too. Jamie'll be your street seller, but I need you to be like, her manager and shit…the girl needs a manager, is all."

◦

SITTING on the stairs outside later after having been booted from my own place by an inebriated and exhausted Paco—he said he'd driven straight down all day and was pooped, as we might put it around these parts—I contemplate my options. I ruminate upon the sliver of moon making its slow trek across the dark sky; I consider abandoning my possessions, Jamie, the beach, and the ocean to hightail it back toward the safety and comfort of home.

But the thought creeps in, the glimmer of hope within a kernel of terror simmering in my stomach like undigested meat, a notion that this situation is a test through which I must pass. The danger of Paco is not so much that I will suffer under his hands, but that I'll shy away from the challenge of confrontation, of standing up to this malicious invasion of what was to be my grand ascendance to a new level of awareness and experience and maturity.

But if what he says is true, this whole misbegotten adventure is about to take a turn for the worse:

Paco has informed me that he plans to meet a connection from Miami in the next day or two, for the real bit of business he has in mind, a much safer and profitable line of merchandise, at least according to him: An ounce of uncut Peruvian flake that has his name on it, merch being ferried to none other than the sleepy tourist town of Myrtle Beach.

"You don't really think I come all the way down here for that cooze, eh? Or to sling dime bags like that dumb-shit Lars?"

"No?"

"Nah. Paco's not that dumb. No, he ain't."

"That's some pretty heavy shit, man."

"Yeah—that's why I need you and Jamie to help me move it," he said before telling me to get my fucking ass out of his crib, which is my crib, though I would call it a pad, man. Whatever a crib might actually be, it sounds to me like where you put a squalling, plump, pink baby Ray-Ray down when he's restless and grumpy and colicky. To get out of the crib is the point of all this, isn't it?

But blow? Don't want to get mixed up in all that. Sure, sure, everyone's doing it, it's no worse than pills—maybe not even as bad, according to this one pin-pupiled, sweaty chick at a bar in the Old Market one night back in Columbia—but damn. Grass is grass. Coke is something altogether different.

Look, I know what I'm talking about—I've been halfway around the block, in a sense. The times I tried the Bolivian marching powder? Stayed up half the night. Slept like hell, once it finally came. Woke up wanting more—which scared the bejesus out of me. Made me remember an *After School Special* I saw about this girl who couldn't stop snorting coke and finally ran out into traffic during an hallucinatory binge (okay, so maybe they didn't get the details of the cocaine high exactly right). I wondered if the authorities weren't onto something, sitting on my bed that morning with a runny nose and an urge to do more of what had caused the condition in the first place. Any substance that makes you want more of it that much makes for a harsh mistress, and not to be trusted.

After a while, I creep back up the stairs and look in to see Paco passed out on the bed, a third of the bottle gone, and half of his bomber sitting propped up on the edge of the ashtray. The roach is so dark with resin it now looks like the cheroot he'd smoked earlier in the evening.

In the evening. What time is it? When and where will I sleep?

The car. The car. The car is the way out, if I want to take it. I'll lose nothing but the clothes I'm leaving behind, a carton of breakfast cereal and the other crap in the tiny fridge, the boom box and the cassettes.

And Jamie.

How can I abandon her to this creep?

The way she looks into my eyes when we're doing the horizontal bop, the way she smells in the morning, the way the curve of her butt looks underneath one of my t-shirts as she stands in the bathroom brushing her teeth: all of these images fill me with anger, make me want to kick the door in and grab the gun and stick it into Paco's face and tell him to get his skinny greaser ass back into his own ride and onto the highway straight out of town.

But I'm not going to do that. If I lose the battle, if I'm not quicker than he is—maybe he's just faking being asleep, expecting me to try such a stunt!—I won't just lose Jamie, I'll lose my life. Dead, over, kaput, *no future-for-you* as Johnny Rotten screams out.

What, then, to do?

Finally I ease on down to the car, making as little noise as possible. I wonder why I've been sitting out on the steps all this time, as though I'm clinging to the danger Paco represents like I'm clinging to the thought that Jamie loves me, that we're going to get out of this together and run away—farther away than I already have—and start a new life over in the next beach town, or wherever the wheel of fate deems to place us. Maybe head west: California, the golden coast, the promised land. First things first, though, and that means to find Jamie, get her side of the story.

And it is thus I feel extra stupid when I go to get in the car and see in the dull white light of the streetlamp that Jamie is curled up in the back seat, fast asleep.

•

I LET her snooze for a while but I can't drift off myself, not at all. Finally I nudge her a couple of times and she rolls over. "What'd he say," she whispers.

"About what?"

"About me."

"More than I wanted to hear."

She sits up and snuggles over next to me. "Paco's a fucken liar. He's a scumbag. Don't believe nothin' he tells you, Ray."

I wonder about all that. But I don't care either way. Jamie's smell is in my nostrils. In spite of the risk, I want to fuck her right then and there in the back seat, like me and Nola-Marie behind the football stadium back home.

I lean over to kiss her deep and long; she responds in kind.

We talk for a while. I give her the details of Paco's plan for us be his street-level operatives all summer here at the beach, moving grams of coke to revelers at the Magic Attic or Mother Fletcher's or the Bowery, to kids on vacation under the pier, to anyone we can find to buy the crap.

"Sheesh," she says. "These guys, they don't quit. Like I told you—if I wanted a job, I'd fucken get one."

But her protestations don't necessarily smack of sincerity. I can see in the gray light of the coming dawn that her wheels are turning, thinking, maybe, about how much money could be made from an ounce of coke that's been stepped on a few times. (I'm hip to such lingo from cop shows.)

"Well, I'm not going for it, babe. And I don't think you should either. I think we should get the fuck out of here while we can."

She folds her arms and looks out the window. "Getting' sick of all you guys telling me what I should and shouldn't do, Ray."

"I only have your best interests in mind."

Actually it's more *my* best interest, which at the moment I wish to be the following: Continuing on with my beach adventure, alternately pumping away inside Jamie or taunting the rubes at the Pavilion, until the season winds down and I make the decision to move on—even if it's only to tuck my tail and skulk back home.

"You're right about one thing: If we was smart," she says, "we'd get outta here before he wakes up."

"Is that smart?"

"Yeah—he's a bitchy little mama's boy in the morning. If I know Paco," and I'm annoyed that she does know his post-sleep habits, "he'll be out until noon, or later. We got to come back, though: He'll find us if we just bolt on outta here. Like he did already."

"Okay, then." We climb out of the back seat and into the front, where I crank the car and ease out onto the avenue.

"Where to?"

She shrugs.

I think about it for a moment. Isolation is what I seek. "I have an idea."

✻

WE HIT 17 and head south, toward Georgetown. I know a nice isolated beach at Huntington State Park, the remnants of some rich motherfucker's estate that, upon his death, was bequeathed to South Carolina to be used as a state park. The property came complete with a weird, Moorish castle of a mansion that Nola-Marie and I visited on our Sun Fun trip two years ago.

It's so early—and so early in the season—that I predict there'll be no one around at all. Jamie and I can walk around in peace, mess around if we want, and think this crazy bullshit through.

I'm going to try again to talk her into getting out today, I've decided. We're going to leave our shit and get out while we can. I'm not dealing drugs all summer; I'm not working for Paco Veracruz and putting my lily-white ass on the line for him. How the fuck is he going to find us, exactly? He's not some crack investigator like Columbo—he knew she was down here, for pity's sake. It's not like Myrtle Beach is a big town or anything.

"You know his name ain't really Veracruz."

Of course. I knew it. "Figures."

"I mean, it's Paco, and all? But his real name is Paco Carattini."

"What's so bad about that? Is that, what, Italian?"

"Nah, Puerto Rican." She says it like *porto-rikken*. "They called him carrot-head back in high school."

"Hah. Good one." I will have to remember this tidbit for a future occasion in which I may be more disposed to insult young mister Paco, rather than offer deference to him and the butt of his gun. "Veracruz sounds better, no doubt. Dramatic. Dashing. Dangerous."

"You sound just like him. You two's made for each other. Hah."

I ignore this ignoble insult, an affront to whatever shred of dignity I might have left, and decide to dazzle her instead with my historical acumen. "Did you know the United States invaded and occupied the Mexican state of Veracruz in 1914? It's the subject of the Zevon that song on the album, naturally."

"Huh?" Jamie scowls at my pedantry. History was my favorite class in senior year at Sims. Mr. Bingham, a hip young guy not that long out of college, with mutton chops and a big mustache, liked to deviate from the textbook quite a bit. If you ask me, he was a little overly enthusiastic with regard to teaching us about American imperial ambitions and incursions into other sovereign nations—he even got in trouble one time when someone complained to their folks that Bingham had said Nixon may have done more than cover up Watergate—old Tricky Dick, Bingham said, may have had a hand in JFK's assassination. That sounded pretty far fetched to me, but damn if it wasn't interesting.

So I relate the story to Jamie as I remember it. "From what my teacher said, a few of our sailors there in the harbor at Veracruz were trying to obtain fuel for a small gunboat, and got taken into custody and then Woodrow Wilson got mad and asked congress if he could invade. They said he could."

"What happened?"

"We bombarded the crap out of the harbor, and two days later moved in. We ended up occupying the city for six months."

Jamie yawns.

"You think Paco knows trivia like that? I mean, about his stylish *nom de guerre?*"

"His *what?*"

"His fake name." I grow weary of Jamie's dumb act, which the better I get to know her, seems like anything but an act. Hard to tell, though. She's sneaky.

"Paco don't know about much other than slinging shit and waving that piece of his around like it was his wee-wee." She looks over at me; I am impressed with her psychoanalysis of Paco's gun fixation, and I give her an appreciating nod.

She continues, "If you're so interested, why don't you ask him? Looked like youse was getting along pretty good in there."

"Maybe I will. Get his mind off this whole coke-dealing thing. I mean, is that what *you* want to get mixed up in?"

She shrugs and looks out the window. "Better than getting some dumb job."

We drive in silence of a couple of minutes. The gray dawn still struggles to break through the overcast sky, and a light mist falls. It feels like ten or even fifteen degrees cooler than this time yesterday; this is the dreariest weather I've yet experienced during this seaside sojourn of mine.

As such, I feel depressed. How and when will I be able to go back to my apartment? That's right—my fucking apartment! Of course, Jamie kicked in that money she ripped from Lars, the dumbass, so maybe it's more hers than mine at this point. But still, I feel a great sense of violation. I'm a man without a home, without a country.

"Is that it?" Jamie points to the sign indicating the turn-in to Huntington Beach.

"Yup."

There's a chain across the driveway, but no one is in the guard shack to deter us from our mission, whatever it is other than just laying low. I get out and drop the chain, drive over it, then replace it. If we get into trouble on the way out, well, we'll just have to get into trouble. What are they going to charge us with? Trespassing on public land? Fuck 'em.

We drive down the short road and then over a quarter-mile long causeway that spans a marshy area. Owing to the weather, I suppose, there is little wildlife activity, in spite of the surroundings and its designation as a viewing area for such creatures. When Nola-Marie and I were here, we saw ospreys and egrets and all sorts of little water birds running around. I was bored with it all then, and only mention it now because it's my only frame of reference with this place.

"Want to walk on the beach?" There is a great, long jetty that juts out into the ocean and provides the entrance to Murrells Inlet, which is just next to the park. "Or check out the mansion?"

"Beach," she says without hesitation. "I need a nap, though."

"You just woke up a little while ago."

"Yeah, well, I didn't sleep much."

"More than I did."

"So we'll both nap."

We take a left at a fork and after a winding ride through scrubby coastal forest for about a half-mile, we come upon the beach parking lot. We get out and both stretch. A boardwalk of a hundred yards takes us past a densely wooded area, and then into the sea oats and the dunes.

I'm cold, and so is Jamie. We walk side by side on the beach huddled together; there is no one in sight on this damp, off-season morning. It feels as though we own this lonesome, windswept stretch of shoreline all to ourselves, a private paradise of surf and sand.

"We could screw out here and no one would know."

"I ain't getting sand in my crack. Forget it."

Jamie peters out, and we're both so cold we only make it a quarter of the way down toward the jetty before she begins whining about going back to the car.

"Look at how far that is, Ray. Gimme a fucken break."

"Aw, you don't know how to have fun." But she's right. My legs feel rubbery from fatigue and tension. I've got a hard knot in my otherwise empty stomach. Probably been there all night, that knot, but I'm only now realizing it here in the gray mist, alone on the beach, a world away from Paco and all his bullshit. "So what are we going to do now?"

"Let's go see your mansion and get some grub." She yawns and rubs her flat belly. She continues talking through another yawn, but I can't understand what she's saying. I don't bother asking her to repeat it.

8

TENDERNESS ON THE BLOCK

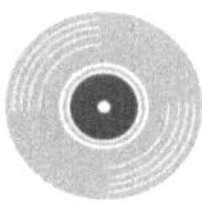

Atalaya, we learn from a brochure, was built fifty-odd years ago by these rich cats to be their summer home. Thing is, the castle is the product not of the rich guy himself—Collis P. Huntington, thus the name of the park—but of his son and his wife, who were rich people by default, I suppose, because when you're that fat, the money rushes down to the heirs like a raging waterfall of cash. Enough, at least, to buy a bunch of beachfront property and build a castle in South Carolina. Of course this area was nothing back then, not like it is now, when people like Sheila can sell off their property and make a nice bundle.

The Huntington scion, Archer, had married a sculptress, Anna Hyatt (herself an hotel heiress, one wonders?) which accounts for all the artwork in Brookgreen Gardens across Highway 17. All of that land used to be theirs as well, but like the state park, they decided to leave this property behind for all the common folk to enjoy.

Hyatt liked to use live animals as models for her pieces, so there are pens at the back of the mansion intended to hold various species, even a bear cage. A bear cage? Someone keeps a bear just for artistic amusement? That's as bad as those poor things you see in circuses. I used to feel pity for all the animals when we would go to Ringling Brothers over at the Southeastern arena every February, when the circus always came through Columbia. I was convinced they were unhappy, especially the lions berated by their cruel master. Daddy always said, no, no, they like their lot in life just fine. If they could talk, they'd tell you so.

I know one thing—these folks that had enough money to buy a beach and build a castle and keep their own circus animals must surely have been happy. Right?

Still barely nine o'clock, we find the parking lot and grounds of Atalaya also deserted. We walk up to the low, one-story building—"designed from memory by Archer Huntington after the affection he garnered for the Spanish style of architecture he'd seen on a European trip," according to the literature. (That rich, smart little turkey. Must be nice like that, having it all.) The building doesn't look like any castle I've ever seen, but it does have a tower jutting up as its main, central feature, maybe thirty, forty feet in height. There is more blah blah blah in the brochure about said tower, which featured a blah-blah gallon water tank that supplied the castle, the height giving it enough blah-blah pressure to supply the whole house.

Jamie has wandered off toward the front of the mansion while I keep reading and pointing; I say *blah-blah* like that because I know that's what she hears. I am known to drone on about information I find of interest, less sophistic than more purely loquacious in nature; as a kid, they called me motor-mouth. The folks say that, once I started talking (a late bloomer, ironically enough, according to my mother), they couldn't shut me up. I guess that's where all the voices came from originally—if they all got tired of my own logorrhea, I'd switch to a new voice. Or at least that's the theory emerging in my mind these last few moments.

"Let's go back and get this over with," Jamie says. "Paco'll be up soon, maybe. We—we got to deal with him somehow."

"Looking forward to it with *enormous* anticipation." I stop and pull her to me. "Again: Why don't we just get out of here? What's he gonna do?"

Fear flits across her face. "I told you: He'll find us."

Tiresome. "But he already knew where you were. That's not finding anybody, that's just showing up."

"You don't know Paco."

"I wish that were true. Let's walk inside, for a little while at least. I want to think things through a bit longer."

Inside Atalaya it turns out the rooms are all pretty small, the study and dining room and various bedrooms now reduced to only the bare brick walls. The castle is really only a big square with a large open courtyard in the middle full of Palmetto trees, and it's hard in this condition to imagine it being the sumptuous home of the well-to-do, though when you look back toward the highway, you see the narrow, old driveway, lined as it is by even more stately Palmettos and gnarled cedars, like many a decent coastal plantation might once have had. Thirty rooms, the brochure says, including sunrooms and libraries and sitting rooms and dining rooms and servant's quarters. I wonder if the hired help lived as well as the bear did.

"We're all alone here, just like those rich people were," Jamie says. "They could do whatever they wanted, whenever."

We peer out an open window in the direction of the ocean, through ornate wrought-iron grillwork oxidized green with verdigris and age. The sky looms flat and gray. It now smells like full-on rain is coming instead of the light mist that hangs in the air. "That's what the big bucks will buy you."

"What's that?"

"Freedom."

"That'd be nice."

"We're freer now than any human beings who ever lived."

"Maybe you are. I can't seem to get there."

Am I? The condition I sought in the first place by coming to Myrtle Beach seems ever more elusive with each passing day. The situation with Paco, and Jamie, is starting to seem as intractable as the life I was leading at Southeastern—only more dangerous, perhaps ruinously so. "What is it you want to get freed from?"

Her expression of wanderlust hardens. "Why you gotta ask so many questions all the time?"

"Just curious, I guess." I feel chastened and silly. *Don't you want to get to know me? And don't you want me to know you?*

"Aw, don't look so hurt."

"Can't help it."

"Big baby."

She shoves me into what the map on the brochure shows us was the servant's dining room. Jamie laughs and scurries on ahead, through the various rooms and around the corner near the ocean-facing, front part of the house.

The *slap-slap* sound of her sandals disappears and silence falls; a chill comes over me once again. Alone again—naturally. "Jamie?"

I follow her path through the rooms until she leaps from behind a low wall and yells out, "Boo!"

I just about shit my pants and tell her so, which sends her into paroxysms of laughter.

"Hide and seek," she says through her giggles. "Let's play hide and seek!"

And so we do for a few minutes, but not like when you're a little kid. She darts in and out of rooms as I try to catch her, teasing me, giggling. But she's too good, and finds every little nook and cranny out of which she can jump.

Finally I corner her in Ms. Hyatt-Huntington's sculpture studio, which has an open skylight letting the light mist fall into the room from above. I grab Jamie and kiss her, deeply, which she seems to respond to like she has over the last month, with passion and sweetness and seeming attraction—until she pushes away and says with a sigh, "You're not like the others, Ray."

"No?"

"Nah, you're a special dude. You're—"

"What?"

"Aw, nothing. Just special, is all. I mean that, okay?" She touches me on the face and gets a look that simmers with sorrow, like she's so sorry—but then she shakes it off and gives me a half-smile.

"What was that look for?"

"Let me do something for you, okay? Just in case?"

"Just in case of what?"

"Well—who knows?"

I don't want to know. And after she sinks down to her knees, looking up at me with that thrilling, willing glance of lustful abandon, I don't much care about the meaning of anything. I just *am* in those moments as she pleasures me—no past, no future.

WE FIND that Paco has trashed the apartment. He's left a note tacked into the door with a steak knife: *You mutherfukers are DEAD.*

"Not a champion speller, this one."

"Shit. Now he's mad."

"Angry? Or crazy?"

"That's the problem—both? Who the fuck knows with him."

"I figured you would, if anyone."

She responds with a quiet *harrumph* and starts picking through the junk on the floor for her clothing and other personal items. I pull the steak knife out of the door and crumple up his poison-pill of a note, expertly toss it across the room into the overflowing wastebasket in the kitchen, where it bounces back out onto the dirty floor.

"If we was smart," Jamie says, flipping a pair of her panties around on an index finger and with a dreamy look in her eyes, "we'd figure out where Paco has the money."

Oh, boy. Here we go. "What money?"

She frowns and shakes her head. "The money for the coke. Ya big dummy."

"Oh." A little thief, this one, just like Paco said, and like I've seen with my own eyes.

In this brief moment, much of what I've felt for her goes flying out the window, and I have what they call in English Lit class an epiphany: She stole from Lars, she wants to steal from Paco, so if we were to stay together, how long would it be before she takes something from me? How long? And what would that theft entail?

Too late—I've already allowed her to steal my heart. Not like Sheila did that night, which seems a long time ago now, but in a different way.

It's all been fantasy though, this whole journey of mine. A living, breathing fantasy, but no more real than some stupid story in a book or on TV. Who, pray tell, have I been kidding about this, besides myself? The fire in my stomach right now is anything but courage—it is abject fear. It is the sense I have to get out of this, somehow. Fuck Jamie, fuck Paco, fuck the beach. They can all have one another.

"That's about as boneheaded an idea as I've ever heard. You see that piece Paco's got under his nasty yellow armpit? Eh?"

"A little boy's popgun."

"Yeah, sure. Tell it to the mortician. Lookit—leave me out of this. I'm ready to pack it in and just split. You could come with me." But to where? Columbia? There's nothing better to do in Columbia except sit around and get high and watch the tube. Why the hell else am I here in the first place, after all?

Jamie, scowling, seems annoyed at my reluctance to acknowledge the brilliance of the idea to rip off her ex-ex-boyfriend. Then: A small sound, a creak from behind me, and the heat in my stomach spreads like wildfires do out west in some dry, thirsty forest full of scrub brush.

"What ya think, Southern boy? You gonna help her rip off my stash?"

Everything's going *tick-tick-tick* like watching a film strip in health class, the one about how guns kill little pink nancy-boys. I turn to see Paco.

He holds the gun leveled right at my gut. "Well?"

"Dude, I don't know how long you've been listening, but—"

"—long enough—"

"—if you heard me, you know I'm not gonna rip anyone off."

He grabs me by my t-shirt, lifting my feet off the ground. "Shut up before you dig the hole any deeper—or else you're gonna need that hole to lay down in."

◦

TOLD TO MAKE myself scarce for awhile, I discover downstairs the latest bit of amazing, invigorating news: Paco has punctured all four tires on my car.

You fucking asswipe son of a bitch… I will kill you, Paco. Dead.

But all my ire and bravado vanishes like smoke, and hot tears come instead. I collapse into the sandy driveway against one of the slashed tires, my head down, my face hidden by my arms crossed over my knees. I'm hungry, tired, scared, frustrated, hopeless. I was going to get in the car and drive away, don't you know. Like I said, I was going to leave them all to their bullshit. And now I don't even have that option. I heave and cry until my stomach hurts. I'm humiliated and impotent.

I have failed.

Upstairs, I can hear the raised voices of Paco and Jamie; I heard what sounds like the smack of an open palm on a face, followed by a small whimper. My teeth gritted, I wonder whether Jamie is a good person. Despite my prior plan to ditch her and get lost, she still retains meaning to me, and the thought of that thug smacking her around makes me want to puke, to fight, to kill that rat bastard.

Instead of killing Paco, I suddenly have an idea of my own, about how I can get rid of this asshole without resorting to such violence. I think of someone that might be willing to help me—and I don't mean Mommy or Daddy, either.

SHEILA'S FACE has gone gray as I lay out the whole situation. She thought I was some nice kid, a college boy from Columbia—and here I am telling her about this coke deal with a Puerto Rican gangster who's threatening to kill me, and everyone around me, if I don't cooperate.

"Jumping Jesus on a pogo stick, Ray. What on earth were you thinking?"

The Olympic Flame restaurant sits empty now that the breakfast rush is over. "I don't know." Hot tears sting my eyes again. I can't cry in front of Sheila. Anyone but her. I clench my jaw and try to breathe.

Sheila is freaked out by it all, worried about being overheard. "Let's get out of here. Bad enough that I'm here with you right now anyway."

"It is?"

"Yeah."

We go across the street and through the two Yachtsman condo buildings toward the beach for a romantic stroll with Sheila, a thrilling ex-lover —or maybe not. The idea fills me with sadness, as does the walk we take onto the pier where this whole adventure began last month. As if to underscore the point even more, I nod at the Vietnam vet with whom I'd shared a beer that first night here on the beach, but he doesn't recognize me.

"Brother," he says, "I sure am hungry."

"Fuck off," Sheila replies, even as I reach into my jeans for a dollar to give the poor guy. "I work for a living."

"*Fah,*" he scowls. "Ya probably never worked a day in your life."

I thought it was the beginning of my real life that night, sitting out in the darkness with a character like him, sharing a drink like a couple of men. The unsavory nature of that activity now seems like nothing more than a precursor to the foolishness in which I now find myself embroiled.

"Only one thing to do, in my opinion. We talk to Carl."

"It's not my first choice. But yeah, that's why I came to you."

She bites her lip and looks out at the whitecaps of the Atlantic. An old man casts a line into the water; he's got an empty bucket at his feet, still waiting for that first catch of the day. "There might be a problem."

I am wearied by this news. "You mean beyond the obvious?"

She gropes for the right words. "Hard to say how much Carl will want to help you, honey."

"I know he's off the force now and all, but listen, I'm not into all this stuff. I just got swept up in it." The excuse sounds lame. If I were a cop, I wouldn't believe a word of it.

She gives me an embarrassed half-smile. "Well—him and me, we been sort-of seeing each other again."

In spite of a quick stab of jealousy I'm glad for Sheila, and for Carl, who looked so sad that morning on the beach. "That's wonderful."

"Yeah, but we both said we had to be honest about each other? About what all we done when we was apart—you understand?"

"You *told* him? About our night together?"

She nods. "I wasn't going to. But we were out drinking, and—it came out."

I suffer a small fit, declaiming that he will surely wring my neck.

"No, no—well, maybe. He was pretty mad that night. I told him it was a big mistake, that it wasn't anything. He kept shaking his head like he couldn't get his mind around it."

"This complicates matters."

"Like he's a saint himself," she mutters with a scowl. "What *he* did when we were still married? Well, never mind. Always different for us women, you know. We're supposed to be little virgins sitting on our hands and waiting all night. Like I said, he's got plenty to answer for. Besides, it meant nothing—that's what I kept telling him. You and me, I mean."

I'm terrified, now, about even being seen with Sheila out in public.

And then I think about her words—that our night held no meaning for her—and I get sad again.

I lean against the weathered wood of the pier railing, the wind whipping my shaggy hair into my eyes. "Well, it was something to me," I say, almost to myself.

She puts a hand on my forearm. "Oh, sugar… my sweet Raymond. You know I didn't mean that. But I had to say it to him, to get him to forgive me. He already has a bunch to forgive anyway. We both do, though. That was my point."

"I hope he got it."

We start back toward the beach in silence. I am stuck now, out of ideas. But what is worse? A bullet from that greaseball, or an ass-kicking by a humiliated ex-cop, pissed about me giving his hot wife the high hard one? These choices—! I never imagined such piteous choices I'd be facing. I only wanted to get away, have some fun, figure out who this is inside my head. And now all this foolishness.

I have to make a move—any move. I don't know how I can face Carl, but I have to. He's my only solution, short of abandoning the car and hiding out until my Daddy comes to pick me up and take me home.

"Call Carl. I don't care. He's my only shot at getting free of this mess."

"I don't disagree. Actually, he's waiting for me back at the motel right now. Come on and let's get this over with."

●

"YOU LITTLE BASTARD." Sitting out by the pool in essentially the same spot where we first met, Carl's face has gone as red as his windbreaker. "You got real nerve showing your ass around here again."

"But Mr. Wilson, it was a mistake. I know that. Sheila knows it, too." But it wasn't—in fact, it was one of the best nights of my life, in a way. If I put it this way to him, though, I'm mincemeat. "She—we were both drunk. I barely even remember any of it."

Talking to Carl out here on the edge of the world, I feel like a fool, an inexperienced, helpless child and a grown man sitting on two cracked, plastic patio chairs by the now-drained pool of the Grand Strand Family

Motel, in which no families will ever again dwell—Sheila says the demo of the building will begin next week.

Grim. Whatever pleasant memories I will take away from this adventure revolve around this decrepit old structure, which soon won't even exist anymore. The sun finally peeks out at least to burn off the gray and the mist, but the light does little to improve my mood.

I can see on Carl's face how sick inside he feels at seeing me, imagining what must have gone on between the love of his life and this skinny, teenaged idiot. Imagining is sometimes worse than actually knowing how a traumatic event went down.

He wipes his face with the back of one huge hand, an appendage that looks in its power as though it could crush my skull. He lights a Camel, cupping his Zippo to block the steady breeze. He snaps the lighter shut and inhales like it's his last smoke before the firing squad. "Here's the deal: You so much as look at her and I fucking beat the ever-loving mud out of you, kid. But you ain't no minor. You're a real man now, ain't you? You could take it, couldn't you?"

"Mr. Wilson—I'm sorry."

"Mr. Wilson's my pa. Call me Carl, boy."

A breakthrough. "And you can call me Ray."

"Sure thing—*boy*."

Okay, okay. "I don't know how all this is going to sound to you, but I'm in a pickle."

"Sheila said you're in some kind of trouble."

An understatement. The story tumbles out. He glowers and shakes his head and looks up to the heavens.

"This asshole, he got the drugs on him?"

"Not yet."

"When's it going down?"

"Not sure."

"Well—if you want me to do something about it, you'd better find out, kid."

That means going back. I have to anyway, don't I? To prove to Jamie that I'm not afraid? Or at the very least—to have the car towed and the tires fixed so I can get the hell out of this? "I'd rather not. But I guess you're right."

Carl's eyes, searching mine. "How do I know this ain't just sour grapes? That he just cheated you outta money, or something?" He smokes and waits. "How do I know you ain't mixed up in this narcotics business worse than you're letting on?"

I search for a way to make it clear. "I wouldn't have come to you, a policeman, if that were true. Do I look like I'm that kind of guy?"

"Looks don't mean shit, boy."

I am desperate to convey my utter sincerity. Whether done consciously or not, my voice breaks in frustration. "I'm not lying about anything!"

He smokes some more and nods before getting to his feet, old knees popping inside his khakis. "Let me make a couple of calls. Listen—there's only so much I can do to help you. I can't guarantee they won't haul your skinny butt in right along with Pablo—"

"—Paco—"

"—or whatever his name really is. You need to understand, I burnt a few bridges in the MBPD, let me tell you. On the way out, you know? Told a few people what I thought about 'em? There's guys that ain't exactly white knights on horseback in that department. Tough hombres, these redneck boys. Not all of 'em are on the level—but some, though." He spits into the empty pool. "I'll tell them you're my cousin's boy, or something." It pains him to say these words. "I'll tell them you're—family. But only because Sheila said you're okay."

I resist the urge to make one of my famous cracks in one of the silly voices, about how he and I are definitely closer in one way than either of us would like to admit. But that would be stupid.

Still—my relief is palpable. "Man—I really appreciate all this." I reiterate an earlier statement: "You have to know I didn't come down here to get mixed up with a bunch of criminals."

"Why *are* you here, Ray?"

The $64,000 question. "God only knows. I thought I knew, but now—?"

Carl looks off into a middle distance I realize must represent his own past. "Getting to go to college—for a lot of us, that's a real privilege." He fixes me with a knowing stare. "Once this is all over with, you get your ass back home, son. Go back to school. Sounds like you maybe already figured that out, but take it from me: nothing down here besides the tourists but miscreants and beach bums. Sheila says you're working as a carny—that can't be what you want out of life."

"Probably not. No."

"Make a real future for yourself. Before it's too late."

I still don't know what, if anything, I do want out of this increasingly weird life—but what Carl says feels accurate. I don't want to end up like some vagrant on a pier panhandling money; I'm not going to end up in jail because some asshole I don't even know wants me to sling dope for him. I'm struck by Paco's stupidity, sort of like driving the ostentatious car— does he think I'm such a pussy I wouldn't just take off the second he leaves again for Jersey?

One fact remains incontrovertible, though: I still want Jamie, in a way —but is it because of the danger she seems to trail behind her? Is it the excitement of being in a real-life cop show? Maybe, but the consequences to the people who get hurt on those TV programs disappear into the ether during the commercial breaks—it's all fiction, and the bullet wounds are red-dye fakes. This world, unfortunately, seems all too real.

Carl tells me to hang while he talks to some people, so I stand and watch as blithe vacationers cruise back and forth on the beach: College kids from up north on spring break; guys who, from their severe haircuts, look as though they are on leave from some military post; snowbirds; young families with little kids. I envy their carefree lives—only days have passed, I realize, since I too felt fancy free, though it seems longer. I need a fucking nap. I need a break.

Carl returns and we discuss matters. We talk about how I need to be careful, about how neither of us knows how dangerous this guy Paco might turn out to be.

"You don't want your little girlfriend to get hurt, either, do you, Ray?"

"No. That I don't." I shake his hand. "I really appreciate this."

He laughs, but devoid of humor. "Don't thank me yet. These situations have a way of turning ugly."

❖

AT THE RISK of seeming melodramatic, I decide to take a moment and call Jenkins while I wait around for Carl's narc buddy. I might as well inform him I'm in trouble—just in case something terrible does in fact go wrong, and I end up either in the pokey, or worse, on a cool slab in the M.E.'s office. I picture an insouciant Jack Klugman whistling to himself and scalpeling into my spongy, gray abdomen. I shudder.

Prepared as I am to leave a message on my brother's machine, dear Jenkins answers his phone. He'll love this conversation. I hope I can get used to liking the taste of the excrement he's going to make me eat.

"Well, if ain't the world traveler."

"Shouldn't you be in class, law-boy?"

He scoffs. "Screw you Ray-Ray. I can take a lunch break, can't I?"

Unresolved anger floods in. "How is she, you little prick? Y'all married yet?"

"She's fine, fine as wine," he says with a touch of jealousy. "What do you want? Money to waste on beach whores and dope?"

"Hey, I work for a living," echoing Sheila's angry sentiment from earlier, though in a more pleasant way. "It's not that. I'm hip-deep in some weird shit. But don't tell Mother and Daddy I called, all right? No use in worrying them until I get this all figured out."

"Why, then, are you calling me with this bullshit? I got my own worries, Ray. You know how hard these classes are? What does 'weird shit' mean? Dare I ask?"

I'm quite sure his coursework is as difficult as he makes it out to be and I tell him so—though my tone remains withering in its condescension. It's a natural instinct when talking to my brother, never more than these days.

In response he is direct: "Let me make something perfectly clear, little man. This act of yours has grown tiresome. I got to say, I'm right sick of listening to Mama whine and Daddy bitch all the time. You gonna come home soon, or what?"

"I should say, old man, that I hope not," I state quite disingenuously in the tried-and-true, clipped British accent. "Doing so would be ghastly, truly ghastly."

And yet all I want, now, is to get out of this grand adventure that has soured on me. Why I can't just come out and say all this to my brother is beyond me—a sense of pride, I suppose, however misplaced. An inability to admit failure. I could still sweep the sordid details under my personal rug. Keep them from knowing the kind of people I've been living and dealing with—my mother would die the second she saw Jamie, not to mention Paco. And, if she knew I'd been in bed with a cigarette-smoking woman like Sheila? I shudder.

"So—what kind of trouble you in?"

I give him a watered-down version of the story, emphasizing the new elements that involve my upcoming performance as a true-blue police informant about to bring down some Latin American drug dealers.

Jenkins DeKalb snorts and guffaws with his patented, adenoidal laughter—an annoying honk—I remember all too well from a lifetime of his juvenile, ribald jokes, disgusting little stories he always found far more amusing than they really were. Never trust a comedian who laughs at his own material. "You just making up crap now, dipshit. What the hell you really want? I don't have any extra cash."

I should have known this was pointless. I trace a finger along the edge of the phone booth. "I just wanted to fuck with you. If you talk to the folks, tell them I said hi, and that I'm doing fine. I'll see everyone —well, later."

"Lord have mercy, boy, you got too much time on your hands. I tell you what, though—Mama ain't finished with you about all this. Daddy's done had to stop her from coming after you about a dozen times."

"No doubt. Look—I'll be home soon. Okay?" I deflate at this admission.

"Your little fantasy not working out?" He snorts again, this time more in disgust than mirth.

I answer quite truthfully, "Not as cool living here as I thought it'd be."

"I could have told you that, shit-ass. People like the DeKalbs don't live at the beach. It's a place to keep a second home, and maybe some rental investment properties. Now while you're farting around down there, I got to go and get ready for Torts." He hangs up on me, abrupt and cruel.

I'm reminded of my father's admonition about not calling him if I finally got into some kind of real trouble. Looks like it will be Carl and Sheila, my beach family, on whom I'll have to count to get my butt out of this.

9

LAWYERS, GUNS & MONEY

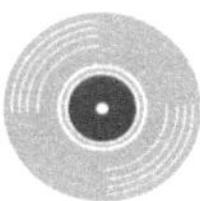

Nothing left to do after the Jenkins call but head back, and so I trudge down the avenue towards "home," such as it is. The Mustang looks forlorn squatting on its four flats; it is an appropriate symbol of my mood. Paco's muscle car still sits parked where it was when I left, so I assume—I hope—the deal hasn't gone down yet.

There's not much I'm sure about, except for this: I want to nail his ass. See Paco with fear in his eyes instead of that wretched, casual bravado. See him frog-marched and shoved into the back of a police cruiser; see him crying for his mama, even. Me shaking the hands of the arresting officers, slapping one another on the back and maybe taking a group snapshot. Case closed.

Then: Carl forgiving me for Sheila. Jamie looking up to me as her white knight. We ride off into the sunset. Maybe take her back to Columbia with me, get her into Southeastern and off the streets with these thugs. A perfect ending.

The fantasy dissipates as I walk up the stairs. I dread seeing whatever it is that awaits me in that dingy little hole of an apartment: a smiling, triumphant Paco, standing over Jamie's beaten, broken body, perhaps. The guilt I feel in this moment for not having protected her from this greaser thug is as a bitter pill stuck in my gullet. A rush of anger wells up inside me, but I try to temper it: I say to myself that I must not provoke him until I can let the cops know, then they can take all the risk in dealing with this turkey.

A different sort of anger hits me as Paco answers the door in his briefs and a stained t-shirt. His eyes are droopy and his face relaxed, as though he'd just awakened. "I was about to put an APB out on your ass, redneck boy." He smiles and glances over his shoulder. "But a good thing you didn't show up five minutes ago, though."

My face flares hot. "Why's that?"

He runs the pink tip of his tongue across his lips. "Me and Jamie, we was busy then. We done now, though—for a while." I can hear the shower running. She's getting cleaned up.

A shock of realization settles over me like a mist. He must have raped her! Or, did he have to force her to do anything? One wonders.

More hurt than angry, suddenly I am forced into Carl's place. Jamie—my Jamie, who admittedly shouldn't be wearing white at her eventual wedding, was doing the nasty with this brutish creep. But it wasn't the first time, right?

Still—I am now like a beast ready to mark his territory, and I make two fists, though I allow them to remain dangling at my hips. Again: Maybe she didn't want to, maybe he forced himself upon her.

"You asshole," I hear myself saying. "

"Unclench them little hands, Ray. You don't own her little white ass—I do. And besides that fact, Jamie told me what a little pussy you was. So much so that—aw." He gives a little frown and looks off. "So much so I don't know I can trust you on this deal. That's disappointing. Maybe even hurtful."

"Oh—you're the one hurt?"

Now he peeks down his nose at me with a squint-eyed look of what can only be termed pity. "Come inside, though—let's us talk it out."

●

JAMIE'S EXPRESSION is one of self-conscious shame as she emerges from the bathroom to see me in the apartment. I glance at her only sidelong, instead directing my gaze to the floor while Paco blathers on and on about matters of trust, and the crude accounting practices of the underground economic activities we're all going to be undertaking.

"I gonna take care of cutting the shit. Don't you worry none about that. After that, though, I gots to get back to the crib, back to unfinished biz back home."

I can't stop thinking about the fact that they were just going at it. The room even smells of their bodies. I am sick. "Whatever."

"It's more than whatever, bro. It's sir-yes-sir."

"Okay, Paco. Sir-yes-sir."

Jamie stands between us, toweling her hair dry. "Look, if Ray don't want to do this—you shouldn't make him."

Paco turns on Jamie, savage, and snatches the towel out of her hand. "You listen to me, you little cooze. You need someone to keep a eye on you. I do it myself, yeah? But I got bigger fish to fry. Long as you send the money—once a week—till the shit is gone, it all gonna be fine, fine like wine."

Now it's Jamie's turn: "Whatever."

"I don' see more enthusiasm outta this little group, I might pull the plug myself on this shit."

Finally I speak up. "But Paco—"

"Yeah, boss?"

"Couldn't you just—?" I try to come up with the right lingo. "*Move* the shit just as easy back home? Easier?"

He checks his watch and starts getting dressed. "I said I had other shit going on, yeah? Besides, I gots people watching me up there, people onto my shit. I don't necessarily mean the heat, either." He laughs. "Down here, people on vacation. They ready to party; they ready to pay to do it. Quick turnover, high profit. You move this stuff in a couple weeks, we can do it all over again, all summer long. High season, all the way to Labor Day."

I'm chilled to the bone at the thought. "Like she said. I'm not sure it's me you want on this deal."

"Look—I ain't no slave-owner like y'all down here. My people do me right, I take care of them. You gonna be paid, cuz."

Paco should go to business school, and I almost tell him so. Jamie rolls her eyes behind him.

A shadow crosses his face, and he licks his lips. "Yeah, that's right. You do me straight, I do it right back the same way." He says this unsmiling and strange. Paco is a liar, I think.

I take a deep breath. "Okay."

"Okay what?" Both he and Jamie shoot me funny, probing looks.

"Just tell me what you want me to do."

Paco gets a big, shit-eating grin. "Like I didn't know that already. Hah."

Jamie gets another look now, a wide-eyed vision of mild shock accompanied by a quick head-shake: *No.*

And yet it is I who should be warning her, but I don't want to, I'm too mad. Jamie's strong-willed—she didn't have to go and fuck Paco again, not if she didn't want to. I'm pissed at her, too, for turning out to be something altogether less than I realized, and for putting me in the middle of this mess. Whatever she gets, she deserves.

●

PACO DISAPPEARS to the payphone down on the boulevard. When he returns, he informs us the deal is set to go down that night. In the interim Jamie and I have not spoken, though several times she's acted desperate to tell me something.

"So where's the deal going down?"

"Good question." Paco strokes his chin in thought. "Right here, huh?"

"I got a better place. This motel where Jamie and—where I stayed before this, it's closed now. Should be deserted."

"A closed motel? What good that do me?"

My mind races. "Because I copied the key to my room."

Paco laughs, but his eyes betray a calculating consideration of my every word. "What the fuck for, whiteboy?"

"In case I ever needed someplace to crash." I struggle to justify it. "In case the money ran out, and I got booted from here. I dunno."

Paco's suitably impressed. "I knew you was a smart kid. You hear that, woman? You wouldn't-a thought of that in a hundred years."

Jamie, sour and closed off. "Shut up. Both of you."

"Let me go check it out, bro." I'm friendly, now, maybe too friendly. But I have to put Paco at ease. I mimic his accent. "We make it all go down real smooth, like peanut butter."

"Okay, little Ray. You go scope it out. Me and Jamie, I guess we'll wait right here." He leers at her again. "Hang out. Ya know."

Hate flows through my veins instead of blood.

❋

I BEAT a path to a different payphone, one more out of sight, where I call Carl. He tells me he's going to bring someone to meet me in order to discuss the particulars, an investigator actually still on the force.

I tell him to meet up on the boardwalk near the Bowery; he advises a half hour until he can get it together.

With that kind of time, there's nothing for it but pay a visit to Mr. Pugliesi. No matter what happens with Paco and the cops, I can't stay around here much longer, and good as Pugliesi has been to me, I need to be straight with him.

He's normally at the Pavilion during the week even without much to be done. I told him one day he should take it easy, that it seems like it would be depressing to hang around this place when the rides are all dark and quiet. "What else I'm gonna do? Play golf? Hah."

Sure enough, he's in his cluttered office, jabbering away on the phone in his native Italian. He waves me in.

He rings off and gestures to a metal folding chair up against the wall. The office smells of history, musty old papers. There are news clippings on the walls, and an old-style circus poster in the corner that promises *Every Thrill Known to Mankind Under Our Big-Top!*

"That from the old carny?"

He looks up at the poster and his eyes crinkle with a weathered smile. "Nah, that was actually a good one." He laughs. "Our little show, it didn't have no big top, no sir."

"Animals?"

"Of course. I always felt bad for them, though, in them cages. We had the saddest bear you ever seen, all skinny and mangy. It was worse when they put the little hat on him… I couldn't never let on how I felt, you know? Not and seem like a man?"

I'm reminded of Ms. Hyatt's bear, waiting his turn in her sculpture studio. We make small talk for a few minutes, he takes another phone call, I stare at my Topsiders.

"So what-a you want, college boy? A raise already?"

"Mr. Pugliesi? I know how this is gonna sound."

His gaze hardens. "What?"

"I'm giving my notice. I have to leave."

He throws up his hands. "What did I tell you? I says to Mr. George, I says, I don't got a good feeling about this kid. He's a-gonna flake out, you watch." He looks disgusted. "I put time into you, Ray. And time is money."

"I know."

"Worst part?"

I wait.

"You're good in the cage. You would-a kept them lined up all summer long."

I feel ashamed. I promised I'd stay the season. I'm a little shit. I want to spill the whole deal, but that will disappoint him even more, me being mixed up with these malefactors. "I'm in a touch of trouble." The words dry up in my throat. "Better for me to go on back home."

"That girl you with all-a time?"

"Sort of. Not that kind of trouble, though." I remember the broken-rubber incident. I think about Jamie and me married with a toddler screaming in its high chair, me working two shit jobs to keep food on the table. I realize in this moment that whatever I feel about her, our future is not with one another—and it makes me sad in a way I can't quite define: Melancholia tinged with a kind of relief. Strange and conflicted.

We could still have some fun together, though. Get a place in Columbia, see where it all leads. Give her a taste of a different life, better people. Give her another chance.

Pugliesi leans back in his chair and fiddles with his mustache. "You gonna go back to school?"

Another thought that fills me with mild distaste, but: "Yeah, I guess so."

"I tried to tell you, this ain't no kinda life for a college boy. No kinda life. For some people, yeah. For me—yeah, sure. But you?" He chuckles. "Nah."

"Fun while it lasted though."

"Yeah, well it's work to me, fun-boy. What about this weekend?"

I consider the possibilities. I don't think it is realistic to expect me even for that, and I tell him so.

Angry now, but it fades to a look of mere annoyance. "That's too bad, too bad. But we'll live. We just a-keep on a-keeping on."

"No hard feelings?"

"Maybe, Ray. But if this the worst prob I got today—it'll be a good day. A good day. I got to tell you, though, when people say they gonna do something, I expect them to keep their word. That's part of being a man."

My cheeks burn. "It just can't be helped. I'm sorry."

CARL and the narcotics officer are both humorless and curt with me; the cop in particular is deadly suspicious of each and every detail. He's plain-clothes and half a head shorter than Carl, but they both share those piercing cop eyes. He's definitely a local, his accent thick as the humidity that's just around the corner from this crisp and bright April afternoon. He's got a legal pad open on his knee as we sit at a table in Peaches Corner; Carl and I sip fountain Cokes but the cop, introduced to me as Lt. Moultrie, doesn't seem thirsty.

"Now I have to assume you're on the level, son, if you come to Carl about all this. Ain't no one mixed up on the wrong side of the narcotics business gonna come to the police, not unless he's got a screw loose somewhere. Or else he's a rat." His smirk is knowing and offensive. "That what you are?"

His eyes are boring into mine, searching for falsehood. I stare right back, but on the inside my heart pounds like the bass beat on a disco track. "No, sir. I mean, yes sir. Look, I got in with the wrong girl. I had no idea what all she was into, otherwise—"

Carl stares through me with barely concealed anger, thinking more about Sheila than Jamie.

"Otherwise I'd have kept my distance from her. And all of this." I hold out my hands. "My father's an attorney back home."

"Don't never know about people, Mr. DeKalb. First lesson: Can't trust anyone no further than you can throw 'em. Especially—" He consults the legal pad. "No bum from up north." He looks over his notes. "If you're such a saint, why didn't you just come to us straight away?"

A good question. "I didn't realize how serious it was. And —he's armed."

"So this girl was dealing marijuana," he says, pronouncing it like *murrahwanna,* "and that didn't seem to bother you none. That ain't serious to you?"

Carl grunts. I sit in silence.

"It's just pot. I mean, it seems like everyone—"

"Well it ain't exactly legal, boy, no matter who all is doing it. I ought to frisk you. See if you got anything on you right now."

My whole head grows hot. "How dumb do you think I am?"

"Remains to be seen, beau." He turns the page of the legal pad to a fresh sheet. "So you say this is supposed to go down, when tonight?"

"Supposedly."

"Well, I need more than supposedly."

"Paco says tonight. All I can tell you."

Carl seems impatient after having allowed his more official counterpart to lead the conversation. "And where, exactly?"

"I had an idea about that. A way for us, for y'all, to control the situation."

And so I tell them about what I said to Paco about the Grand Strand, the key, the whole bit. The men look at one another, nod their heads.

Carl says, "I'll go get a key for you, Ray. But listen—"

"Yes, sir?"

"We got to keep Sheila from knowing about all this, least till after it goes down. She ain't gonna cotton to no funny business at her Daddy's motel— even though it ain't exactly hers anymore, any more than it's his. Got it?"

I am a cool customer, as much as possible considering the level of comfort between me and Carl over his precious Sheila. "Not like I'm planning to see her again."

Carl scowls. "Damn straight you're not."

Moultrie looks from me to Carl and back again, his cop wheels turning and trying to parse our enigmatic remarks to one another. If he's a good cop, he realizes there's some subtext to our body language.

"You say this Carattini character is armed?"

"Yeah—a handgun he keeps in a shoulder holster."

"Caliber of the weapon?"

I shrug and look at Carl. "Like on TV. Bigger than some, not as big as Dirty Harry's."

"Kind of square looking?"

"Sure."

"A .45, probably."

Another shrug. "All the same to me."

"That's right—they are the same," Moultrie says. "All of 'em will put you in the ground faster than you can say toot-sweet."

A chill runs through me, and I'm no more optimistic about all this than before I called Carl. "If I don't get back soon, Paco'll get squirrelly, you know?"

We leave the diner and I look around, nervous as hell.

"You don't think you been followed, do you boy?"

"I doubt it," I reply, quite unsure. "Paco and Jamie have been busy."

"Ah-hah," Carl says. "Now I see all this pretty clearly. You, Lt. Moultrie?"

The cop's laugh burbles up sardonic and bitter. "Yeah, yeah I think I do. Well—whatever your motivation, boy, you done a good thing helping us get this junk off the street."

By *junk* I don't know if he means the drug dealers or the dope itself. And furthermore, my motivation is what it is: To save my narrow small-town ass, and that's about it. I don't care if people snort themselves to death: If God exists, then for whatever reason it is He who gave us our free will, even if it ends up used to destroy ourselves. "Consider it my gift to the Myrtle Beach police force."

"A gift?"

"You guys bring him in and that's that, after which I get to walk away. Right?"

Carl and Moultrie look at one another not with humor but grim anticipation. "Anything you ain't told us?"

I shake my head. "Like Carl knows—I'm a college student. I'm not like Paco."

His face pinches with cynicism. "You might want to walk away. But depending on what goes down, you might not get off clean like that. Not with people like this. Not with money on the line. You got a lot to learn, DeKalb. And you're liable to learn too much tonight if we ain't careful."

PACO, having gotten back into the bottle of whiskey, is sleeping yet again. Jamie sits in a chair, rocking her bare foot back and forth.

"It's all set," I tell her. "I checked and my key still works. Place is like a mausoleum. Perfect."

"You ain't never said anything about no key to the motel."

"I figured what you didn't know wouldn't hurt you."

She's biting her lip. "This whole thing, that's what I don't know, Ray. About none of this."

"What don't you know? Which one of us you like fucking more? I mean, between me, and Paco, and Lars… you're getting around." I start to call her a cooze, just like Paco. But I'm not him. I'm a nice guy from Tillman Falls, where we treat our women with respect.

She starts a little at the mention of Lars. Her cheeks flame red. "It ain't like that, Ray. It—he—"

"Fuck you, Jamie." My voice breaks like it did when I was thirteen, going through the changes. It is a funny and humiliating voice to be sure, but quite involuntary. "I thought you said I was special."

"I'm *sorry*," she says in a harsh whisper. "I'm—I'm just scared about all this. What was I supposed to do?"

"Nah, nah," I growl in an Edward G. Robinson, gruff hard-case of a voice. "Don't worry, doll-face. We'll make us some scratch, blow off this place, maybe hit Vegas. Maybe hit the big time, sweets." I am so disingenuous I want to puke.

Jamie looks stricken. "I'm sorry I got you all mixed up in this. Look— don't come tonight. Just wait here, okay?"

"I can't do that, Jamie. And stop saying 'I'm sorry.' You sound like a broken record."

"That's all I got left to say to you."

I notice Paco staring at us from the bed. Mocking my natural accent: "You-all get us squared away?"

"Motel'll be perfect. We keep this place clean," I explain, "and that way we can sling the blow from here and not worry about anything. That sound about right?"

In actuality, it sounds stupid and suspicious, but not to Paco, who nods through a yawn. "Good thinking." He stretches with nonchalance. "That's it then. Tonight's the night. Eight o'clock sharp, unless old Lupe gets stuck in traffic. Which he *won't*," Paco emphasizes. "Dude got to turn it around and head straight back to Miami. Rough life, being a coke mule. Lotta driven'.'"

I go to the front window, where I look as blasé as I can while my eyes scan up and down the street for the undercover guy, who Moultrie said would pretend to do yard work down the way at an empty house for sale.

I see the guy, in shorts and a t-shirt, leaning against a rake and looking in the direction of the apartment. Discreet, I pretend to reach up and scratch my chest—I flash him four fingers, then another four.

The cop nods and goes back to raking the non-existent leaves in the yard, and I let out the breath I didn't even realize I'd been holding. I turn back to Paco, but he isn't even looking at me, instead focusing on the joint he's rolling.

Jamie stretches and yawns, a bit too forcefully in my opinion. "I gotta get outta this dump. Go to the beach, or something."

Paco and I exchange a look. "The beach?" he asks.

"Yeah." Knowing Jamie all too well at this point, I wonder what she has in mind. "What the hell for?"

"Nothing," she says, irritated, pulling on a sweatshirt over her tank top and sliding into her flip-flops. "I just need some me time before all this gangster crap. Makes me nervous as all get-out."

She's halfway out the door before Paco says, "Well, you just be back here in a hour or two. You hear me, bitch?"

She flips him off. "Whatever."

And then she's gone. Paco and I are alone. He looks at me, hard. "What up wit dat girl?"

I shrug. "Women. Can't live with them, can't shoot them."

Paco busts a gut at that, and we share a laugh as though old buddies.

"You got that right, *man*. Sometimes, though?"

"Yeah?"

"You *can* shoot 'em—if you have to."

I go stare into the empty refrigerator for a while, but no food magically materializes, and even if it did, I couldn't eat.

"Wish there was a TV or something in this dump. You really low-rent, son, you know that?"

"How about some music?"

"Good idea. Here—toke on some of this and kick back for a while."

I start the Zevon tape where I'd last left off, which, as it turns out, was near the end. The last song. *"Dad, get me out of this."* I get a cold spike of fear in my gut.

○

THE TIME IS NIGH. We've driven over in Paco's ride and parked on a side street behind the Sea Nymph or maybe the Sea Gypsy—I'm too nervous to even notice. As a group we mosey on over toward the darkened Grand Strand Family Motel.

"Now you little fucks are gonna hang on the sidewalk. Gimme that key, Ray."

I hand it over to him. "Number seventeen, facing the beach. Should be deserted as hell." A blatant lie, having seen no less than three different guys walking along who are most definitely the heat—though Paco seems oblivious. The dumbest fucking criminal in history, I decide. This will be all too easy.

Once on the Boulevard, Paco scans the street, which is quiet. He sees a van parked a little ways down—a tan, beat-to-hell Dodge with an elaborate, custom paint job depicting an impossibly buxom Latino babe lolling on a sunlit, fantasy beach—and flicks his Bic lighter on and off three times. The headlights on the van flash and go dark again.

"Stay right over there," Paco instructs, a thumb thrust in the direction of the Holiday Inn down the street. The other amusement park, the one with the big roller coaster they call the Swamp Fox, looms in the distance. I wanted to get around to riding that thing one of these nights, but this time of year the park is only open the same time the Pavilion—and that means I'm at work and can't have any fun.

I'd kill, now, to be able to get back into the dunking booth, but that's all over with now. Just like Jamie and me, I suddenly realize. I want to kiss her one more time; perhaps I will as soon as Paco and his connection disappear.

Paco lopes across the street as his hook-up, a shorter and fatter Hispanic youth, climbs out of the van and angles toward him, jaywalking in the direction of the Grand Strand Motel, carrying a small briefcase as though he's Paco's public defender.

"Seventeen? I thought you was in fifteen when you were over here." Jamie is frowning, biting her nails. "That ain't right."

My heart thuds. "But of course it is," I say in a passable Sean Connery brogue. "You were so inebriated you just don't remember, lassie." My forced humor does little to convince Jamie. I didn't even think about the fact she would remember such a detail; Carl brought me a key to one of the ocean front units, which was all I specified. I am shaking with fear now, shifting back and forth on my two anxious feet.

Jamie, too, seems fraught with worry. "I just don't know, now, about all of this. Get—get out of here, Ray. Please."

I utter a short, barking laugh. "We do what he wants, then we can, you know, be together again once he's gone. Maybe we can skim some of the money like you did before, you know? How the fuck's he gonna know?"

Jamie cries softly, wiping at her eyes with a hand half-covered by the long sleeve of her Myrtle Beach sweatshirt, which features a cheap screen print of a middle-aged couple happily shagging in their penny loafers. I bought her the shirt one night when we were walking around and she was cold. It made me feel grown up at the time, caring for my girl.

"What is it?"

"Nothing—just scared." She looks terrified, a Jamie I have heretofore not encountered. I'm more worried than ever.

"Maybe at the end of the summer—well."

"What," she asks, looking around, wide-eyed.

"You could come back with me. To Columbia. I'm gonna go back to school."

Distracted, she watches Paco and his friend like a hawk. "Sure. That sounds great for you."

Paco and his connection have met up with one another in the motel parking lot. They both glance around, exchange a handshake and a one-armed man hug. They disappear further into the shadows towards the ocean, then out of sight.

Once they're gone, Jamie starts across the street. I grab her arm. "Where the hell are you going?" No voices now other than my own scared, little-boy squeak.

"I—I need to—ah, shit, Ray!"

"What the hank is going on here?"

She doesn't get a chance to tell me, but I find out soon enough. Just as Carl and Moultrie pull up in front of us in a tan sedan, cops appear coming from every direction.

Jamie blanches as Carl jumps out. "Get in, both of you," he demands.

"Ray—you little shit."

I wrench open the back door, but Jamie won't budge. She jerks free of my grasp and hauls ass across the street, toward the motel.

"Jamie!" I yell. "You don't understand—"

"Let her go, DeKalb," Moultrie barks. "She was gonna be charged anyway. Let it play out."

"That wasn't part of the deal!" I take off after her; she disappears down the alley.

"*Don't*, Lars!" I hear her scream. "There's cops!"

Lars?

Lars?

Oh, no, Jamie. What have you done?

Moultrie and the rest of the cops go tear-assing through the parking lot, guns drawn, the lights of their rollers splashing blue all over the motel buildings; one of them tackles me and we both go down onto the asphalt. It is then I hear the crackling of gunshots, and aggrieved shouting of voices familiar and otherwise.

I piss my pants, right there in the parking lot, and cry out one last time for Jamie.

※

SITTING NOW in the police station, I find after a long and humiliating time that I'm finally able to stop crying.

When I called my father, it took several unintelligible moments of choked, closed-throat weeping to even get the words out. "Please, come get me," I finally croaked. "Please, Daddy."

He asked over and over again what was wrong, but I didn't have the words for what had happened, not yet. I didn't have the ability to tell him that I had gotten my new girlfriend killed.

It's true. The shoot-out, precipitated because of Jamie herself, as well as her apparent one and true boyfriend, took her life. Her nervous attitude now clear, as is the layer upon layer of duplicity of which she was capable, Jamie had conspired not with me or Paco, but none other than Lars Dammick.

Lars, it seems, had been waiting in the shadows of the alleyway that runs down the side of the Grand Strand Family Motel, ready to rip off Paco all over again. As near as anyone can tell—Lars came away unscathed, though Paco, like Jamie, is cold and dead in the morgue—Jamie tipped off her old boyfriend about the big coke deal the day before, and he'd busted ass back down from Jersey. He'd lain in wait after meeting up with her this afternoon—that had been her big beach trip, her me-time that she needed. It was the last me-time she'd ever have, now.

Jamie—I'm so sorry. I wonder if she can hear me; I wonder if even then she would be placated by my pathetic apology. Somehow, I doubt it.

Daddy and Jenkins show up just after one o'clock that morning. I listen to them speaking with Moultrie outside the interrogation room where I'd made my official statement.

"What are the charges against my boy," my father says in his most officious lawyer's voice.

"None, Mr. DeKalb. He's the one that brought this case to us. Let me take you through it as best we understand the facts at this time."

I can't help it—I start crying again, and I can't stop for a long time, especially when I'm finally let out of the room, and I see the faces of my family waiting for me: A scowl and piteous head-shake from Jenkins; a wet-eyed look of concern from dear old Dad.

"Where's your car, Ray-Ray?" is all he asks. "Where are your things?"

I'm humiliated all over again. All I want to do is get the hell away from Myrtle Beach, but with the vehicle in its current condition, I realize with a start we won't be able to depart until they can buy a set of tires.

"Can't we just leave it?" I sputter. "Can't we just leave all of it here?"

Jenkins and Dad look at one another. "No, son. We can't just leave your car."

***

WE ARE all night in the police station getting things sorted out. Lupe Marzol is superficially wounded, I find out, and is so far refusing to talk. Standing outside the interrogation room, I see an unharmed Lars Dammick being led down the hallway, his face a mask of fading bruises from what I assume is the beating Paco intimated having given him back in Jersey.

As Lars and his escort approach down the long passageway, the harsh fluorescent lighting, along with the late hour, makes everyone look hollow-eyed and bluish-gray, as though we've all been embalmed. I inquire about the charges against Lars, and they are serious: Possession of an unregistered firearm, trespassing, other minor infractions. Moultrie says that Lars shot Paco point blank before dropping his firearm and giving himself up to the authorities.

"Murder, then."

"No," he says. "I mean, these boys was up to no good and all, but it really was self-defense. Carattini shot first." He makes a thumb-and-forefinger weapon with his right hand. "The girl," he says matter-of-factly, as though I would have already forgotten that grim detail. He swings his arm around in a short arc, pointing the imaginary firearm at me. "And then he fired at Dammick—but he missed."

I am overcome with rage at the stupidity and duplicitous nature of this group with whom I have become so disastrously entangled. "This is your fault," I scream as Lars and his escort draw near. "You fucking asshole!"

Moultrie grabs me by the arm with an iron, impregnable grip.

"That bitch ass *mother*fucker killed her, dipshit! And so did *you*—!" Dammick's eyes blaze at me. He screams and lunges, but the cop leading him down the hallway throws Lars against the wall and subdues him. "The second he saw me come out, he fucking plugged her, that spic *bastard.*"

I observe, then, that Lars, too, weeps bitterly for Jamie, his face a mask of psychic pain. Another dismal epiphany: I think he loves—loved—her. And now he will live forever with the image of her lying there dead on the ground—as will I, even though I only saw her broken, small body carried out underneath a pink, stained sheet, followed by that of Paco's corpse felled, I now understand, in anger—in street justice.

No justice, no peace I think, even though in this context, the revolutionary call to arms has absolutely no meaning.

WHAT I SUSPECT I will end up remembering most about the next morning is the *scratch-scratch* sound of Daddy's gold Cross pen as he writes out the check for my new tires at the Goodyear place—the pen set was a gift from me last Christmas. The sound will be burned into my mind, as well as the weather on this bright morning: It is downright hot today—it feels as though the muggy Carolina summer has already begun.

But I will not stay to see the beach explode into life with happy, untroubled people; my now-ignominious vacation from reality is over.

After collecting the rest of my possessions—I have to go and vomit in the bathroom in the middle of sorting out my stuff from Jamie's, which a waiting police officer will hold onto until if and when someone from her family comes to collect the clothing and other objects—we start back toward home on 501, and in Conway turn hard left onto to 378, which will bee-line us back through Columbia. Jenkins drives the Mustang back, following us the whole three-hour drive to Tillman Falls. At first, I demand to drive my own car, but Daddy just shakes his head no, no, no.

The only things of mine that I consciously left behind were the frightwig and ridiculously outsized sunglasses I wore in the dunking booth.

Those pieces of my past seemed as silly as children's toys, and when I noticed them on a chair in the kitchenette, they filled me shame.

I made sure, though, to pop the Warren Zevon tape out of Jamie's boom box. Don't know when I'll listen to it again, though. Just wanted to have it—the soundtrack to my grand and ruinous adventure.

We don't even speak for about forty minutes, Daddy and me, until we stop at a place called Carraway's, a general store on a curve in the middle of nowhere.

"Son," Richard DeKalb finally says. "You must be starved."

I tell him no, even though I am ravenous. I am a murderer; how can I possibly eat?

He and Jenkins go inside to get the inexpensive hot dogs that a sign out front trumpets, and I wander over to a small petting zoo set up two-dozen yards from the store. Sad-eyed deer look out at me; I blink back tears yet again, even though I must surely be all cried out by now.

The DeKalb men come back out eating their hot dogs and drinking Cokes; they confer in a huddle like the lawyers they are.

As I wander up, hands jammed in my pockets and my head down, I hear Jenkins saying, "We'll be able to keep it quiet, Daddy. Ain't no one gonna know, not in Edgewater County. How would they? When Ray-Ray goes back to testify, it'll be long after you done won the race."

"I hope you right, son. I hope you right." Daddy's worried about his campaign for the State House.

My stomach drops into my feet: However I feel about all that bullshit, the thought of this mess ruining his dreams makes me sick and ashamed.

"This is what happens," Daddy says under his breath, unaware I can hear him, "when you live a carefree life. Life is not like some game. When you a little boy, playing games outside in the yard?" He turns and notices me, locking eyes. "You don't realize how easy it is—easier than you think —for people to get hurt."

Once we got to Columbia, it was tough passing by the Southeastern campus; in that moment the defeat and stupidity of my sojourn along the shore truly hit home. But worse was walking into the house and seeing my mother sitting there, her own face pinched and tear-stained, looking as though she'd aged a hundred years since I last saw her a mere six weeks ago. I try to tell myself that she doesn't look that bad, but I can't deny she does, and all my fault.

My fault. There are dead people now, and it is my burden, even though Carl and Moultrie told me this might have happened anyway because of Jamie's disastrous subterfuge, which, they also reminded me, started me down my sorry path in the first place.

I accept none of it. I stare into my boyhood bathroom mirror at a hollow-eyed version of my once youthful visage, and the only palliative I can come up with, at least in the near term, is my parent's liquor cabinet, which I raid as soon as Jenkins leaves and they have gone to bed.

THE SUMMER ROLLS on long and brutal, hotter than any I can remember. I get a job at the Green Briar Country Club bussing tables in the restaurant; by July, I have become a waiter, and I make great money, especially on the weekends. I save up almost enough to pay for the fall semester like I'd promised I would, but in the end Daddy writes the check and tells me to hold onto what I've earned so I don't have to work while I'm in school.

I am in contact any number of times with the MBPD about the case; Lars, as it turns out, has outstanding warrants back in New Jersey for a veritable laundry list of crimes both petty and otherwise, so he'll be lost in the system for who knows how long, which comes as a relief: I worried he might come after me one day, and I suppose he still could.

No charges end up being filed against Lupe Marzol, however, other than trespassing and the possession of his own small handgun.

"What about the cocaine?"

"Turned out they wasn't no drugs on him or anywhere in his van," Moultrie tells me. "Just a Zip-lock full of talcum powder and baby laxative." He utters a short bark of a laugh, one bereft of amusement. "Thing was, Carattini didn't even have enough money to buy that much dope in the first place, either."

"Are you kidding me?"

"This whole thing was one big screw-you, every one of them trying to pull something off on the other. Most messed-up bullcrud you ever seen.

Them people died for nothing, Mr. DeKalb. But you couldn't've known that was gonna happen like it did. I know it probably don't seem like it—but you still done the right thing."

Somehow I don't feel any better. But I bet you could have guessed that. Jamie haunts my dreams; I drink and drink, but she still creeps in there, almost every night.

Finally I dream of the morning at Atalaya, and Jamie in this one tells me that *it's okay, it's okay*. I'm no dummy; this is only my conscience trying to clear itself, lest I lose my mind.

Who was really at fault here? Didn't I try to help her, not hurt her? Maybe her death was the price of her dishonesty—but this is not for me to judge.

The summer wanes. As I said, I have enrolled in Southeastern for the fall semester, but my parents are making me commute from Tillman Falls this time rather than moving back in with Chris, which in some ways is fine: To go back to that life would stoke the guilt, which has already begun to feel like the eternal flame on JFK's grave. The days of living with Chris represent a time before all my bad decisions, a blithe era of innocence, when I didn't know how good I had it.

Oh, but wasn't I miserable and lost before? And if so—what am I now in the wake of the horror I found myself caught up in as my reward for seeking some greater truth through experience and exploration?

I do not know; I may never find out.

◦

Septemberism is here and everyone is excited about Redtails football and the cooler weather and the new semester. I go to class, I eat, I drive the half-hour back home to Edgewater County. Some afternoons I spend drinking beer down in the Old Market; some I drift idly away by walking, walking, walking, endless strolling back and forth across campus.

Every now and then I catch a glimpse of Jamie out of the corner of one eye, but, as none of those girls turn out to be her. Not by a damn sight.

The nightmares have tapered off, at least.

But not the culpability. That, I fear, may linger for a long time. I should talk to someone about it. But I don't. I just pretend, instead, that everything is fine.

Kenny-Ken has now graduated from Marion Sims High and moved all the way out to California; he's living his dream, going to UCLA film school. When I talk to him he's breathless with excitement, says I ought to come out there and visit.

"The women are all unbelievable," he says. "Place is lousy with gorgeousness and gorgeousity made flesh, oh my brother."

I try one afternoon to get stoned with Chris and his girlfriend Rachel, a pretty sophomore from a rich Charleston family; as soon as the buzz hits, though, all I can see is Jamie's dead face, even though I only knew her as a living, breathing, laughing girl who I thought cared about me. I start shaking inside and can't stop for a long time; I scare the shit out of my friends, who want to take me to the hospital, but I don't let them. If I'm having a heart attack, I want it to come so I can be done with it all. But the event passes, along with the buzz, and I decide to give up puffing grass.

One afternoon, a gray one, I find myself waiting at the train crossing as the freight cars rumble by and the drizzle settles over me; it is almost exactly like that day back in the spring, though this time there is no Asian girl with whom I can have an unsatisfying conversation. I am alone as can be.

The powerful rhythm of the passing cars fills me with dread; I wonder if it wouldn't be better for the train to derail and crush me under a hundred thousand tons of steel. I try to will such an outcome for a brief moment, but consider the consequences of such action. Who else would be hurt? How many would die? And how many would be left behind to wallow in the grief and anger at me for my callow, selfish behavior?

As if one had the power to derail a train through the force of desire itself.

As if.

Finally the last car rumbles past and I cruise down the hill and hang a hard right into the Market proper, thinking about a cold beer and maybe a hot dog at Frank's. The train sounds its horn farther down the tracks; it is as a mournful clarion call, a signifier of an ineffable yearning that consumes me more with each day—different, though, from the spring time, when I sought to find something new and unusual and alive; now this feeling wells up in the service only of escaping rather than seeking, and it makes me sad, so sad.

If only we could know what life had in store for us, would it not be easier? Wouldn't that make everything go down smoother, having fore-knowledge of the consequences of our choices, our actions?

Bitter, I scoff and spit onto the dirty sidewalk. If God were here, I suspect he'd reply, *But Ray-Ray, what would be the fun in that?*

EPILOGUE: THE WIND

By the time I pull up in my rented Lincoln Town Car, the Galivant's Ferry Stump Meeting, an enduring and important political event in South Carolina, is well underway. I was pissed after I flew into Columbia and discovered the pathetic selection of luxury vehicles the rental agency had to offer; seems like a toy compared to what I've got in my garage back in Malibu—not to mention at the spread in Montana.

But that's neither here nor there, and while this is a big day for my brother, all I can think is this: Myrtle Beach may be twenty miles farther east, but I can already smell the ocean, I can taste the salt in the air, and feel the loose white sand between my toes. I can see Jamie's face; I can feel Sheila Wilson's feminine shape beneath my own, her legs wrapped around me, my being suffused with the rich smell of her body, which I conflate now in my memory with Jamie's own unique scent. So much time has passed I can barely remember the difference between the two women, even though that gulf was as wide as the ocean beside which I made love to them both.

Maybe that smell on the breeze isn't the ocean but instead the chicken bog or barbecue or perhaps the bullshit being thrown around by my brother, who's being anointed today to serve as the candidate to succeed good old Fritz Hollings in the U. S. Senate now that the enduring, venerable lowcountry politician has decided to retire.

And even though he's a Democrat, Jenkins has done all right in this reddest of red states in his one term as *gub'ner*. Until, that is, he advocated getting rid of the stars and bars from the State House grounds. I don't think he's got a snowball's chance in hell for the Senate now, not after trying to take down the battle flag. But you never know. It's a new century, now, and times have changed, even in a place like South Carolina.

I know what you're thinking—at least one of Daddy's boys made it, right?

Ah, Daddy. It was as painful as it ever is to see him yesterday, less so for me than for Jenkins, whose heart is stabbed over and over by the fact that our father doesn't even remember his own son won two terms as governor, and has no idea that he'll be our next Junior senator from the great state of South Carolina. The early-onset Alzheimer's came on retired State Senator Dick DeKalb fast, so dreadfully fast, and while he was lucid enough to see Jenkins win the gubernatorial campaign, since then my father has drifted farther and farther away from us.

In weak moments, I fantasize that Daddy hears my voice coming over the television speakers and somehow knows it's his son—but since I don't sound anything like myself when performing, that result is unlikely.

Mama, who's in great shape—as her sixtieth birthday present to herself back in '90, she checked in, finally, and got off the booze—says Daddy knows more about the world than he lets on. He always did, I think, but I never tell her that because I'm not sure myself what I mean by it. Whatever I say to her, or to him, it is always in my own voice; I involuntarily drawl a little when I speak to my parents, as though in their voices I find the echo chamber that is my past, my childhood.

Yes. My voice; my many voices. How right old Pugliesi was, and even Paco Veracruz, when they both wondered about my future in comedy. Not comedy per se—but oh, how the voices ended up changing my life.

●

MY GOOD FORTUNE in LA did not come instantaneous, of course. Whose does?

I didn't even go out there because I thought I had a future in show business—I went because good old Kenny-Ken had implored me to do so. Yes—I just up and left Southeastern again, roughly a year after the Myrtle Beach debacle.

What can I say? I took a long time in healing—in some ways, I still haven't. Lars was partially correct—people lost their lives, and in no small measure because of my actions. I still struggle with this guilt, to this day. It won't quite leave, not completely. My therapist says the only thing you can do is mitigate those feelings, not erase them.

So anyway, Kenny called one day in late 1979 and said, "When are you coming out, dude?" I told my parents I was going to visit him in LA over spring break, but once out there I never came back. Not for a long time, at least.

I was a bad son. But they'd come to expect it by then, I think.

I had many adventures; none involved death. Met a hold-over hippy girl or two, had many good times along the way. Hung out on the beach a lot—Venice, sometimes farther north. Lived up in Santa Cruz for a while, checked out the Bay Area; worked shit jobs to keep a headstash together. I existed from moment to moment—I even started doing many of the substances that I had previously forsaken. I was moving backwards.

I came back to LA in '81 after my Santa Cruz old lady, a Deadhead who called herself Janice Sunflower, got sick of me moping around all the time in a tenebrous funk. By then, Ken had started making his student films, and had a spare bedroom I could occupy.

I cleaned myself up. Said, for what did Jamie die? For me to learn nothing at all? For me to go down the same sorry road? I became determined to walk the straight and narrow, make something out of myself. Still didn't know what, though.

Until: I helped Kenny out by acting in a couple of his productions, and doing something he called looping. He made a comedy short; I dubbed in the voices of every character, each one more outrageous than the last. I got "work" on other student films. Someone said, you know, you're good. You should do comedy.

Later, as providence would have it, Ken wrote a hell of a screenplay as his senior thesis, an edgy, balls-to-the-wall action picture called *BloodGun*. It sold to Fox; it put him on the map. In one of those Hollywood vagaries, however, an actual movie never came out of Ken's script, but it did lead to other things—and not only for him. Ken's agent turned me onto my agent, and I still have her to this day. She's a real dragon queen—she gets me mega-bucks for what I do.

And so: Voiceover work on commercials and low-budget Saturday morning cartoons became my calling card. The voices—none of them my own—established me as a real go-to guy when they needed just the right super villain or cutesy animated animal.

By the time I signed on a few years later as a regular cast member on one of the first adult primetime animated series since *The Flintstones*, I was doing all right indeed. I had only had my first divorce by then, and was lucky enough to have gotten it out of the way when I did: I had no idea how much money I would make later on.

The second divorce? My lawyers had been persuasive enough to talk me into a pre-nup with the fellow actress who was, oh, twenty years younger than my withered, fat ass. File it under foregone conclusion. I'm just lucky to have stayed out of the tabloids.

But anyway: My TV series, now fifteen, sixteen years down the line, is still going strong, and if it isn't quite as popular as in the beginning, it's still a top twenty-five show on most weeks—sometimes higher, sometimes lower, but pretty damn stable as far as these things go.

The other cast members and me all make more money than God, it seems, for what we do—and among the family of actors we're more than fortunate. They can't just replace us—I alone do two major characters and a half-dozen supporting ones, as well as a variety of celebrity imitations when we're skewering some of our fellow Hollywood types. Without us— without me, especially—there's no show, not now that it's become a national institution. You know what they say about whores, architecture, and eventual respect, including Emmys.

The last contract negotiation bought and paid for the Montana spread; how long the show will go on is anyone's guess. Doesn't matter now— royalties alone will keep me flush pretty much forever. I'm set. A long way from both Edgewater County and Myrtle Beach, I have come.

And once I did get on my feet and settled down into this crazy career, I reconnected with my family back home, tried to make up to them the way

I'd behaved. We've all been good friends ever since. More good fortune. I don't deserve it.

❉

I FINALLY MAKE IT 'BACKSTAGE' at the Stump Meeting, and wave to my brother as Jenkins smiles his patented, toothy, aw-shucks grin. He introduces me around to great acclaim; Senator Hollings pretends to know who I am, but it's clear he's only being polite. Jenkins and his lovely wife Sherilyn—they met after Nola-Marie fell for one of her T.A.s at Southeastern; she's had her own career as a powerhouse, progressive attorney in her own right—both exude grace and authority.

Jenkins is far from the man I thought he would become—like I said, he even stayed a Democrat, for god's sake. He speaks with careful articulation, his accent the same, only flattened out a bit. (Not much—just a bit.) He's trim and tan; he's like a different person, almost.

But so am I—except, maybe, on the inside.

Show business: it's like Pugliesi warned me, it's brutal, not for the faint of heart, a cold-blooded dance of ego and expectation and dreams dashed upon the jagged rocks that comprise the craggy bottom line. Even if the show is canceled tomorrow, though, I'll always have work. Now that computer animation is so cheap, there's no shortage of talking-animal and talking-car and talking-object movies, so my services should remain in comfortable demand.

The perks of being an actor—although in my case only a voice actor— have been numerous. Money, a high degree of freedom, a few nice lovers and friends along the way. Some people, not so nice. But you take the good with the bad in life.

A highlight? I once got to hang with Warren Zevon, back in the mid- 90's when my burgeoning celebrity allowed me to slink my way backstage at a club date. I told him how much *Excitable Boy* had meant to me many years ago, how it had provided the soundtrack to a difficult time in my life.

He thanked me, of course, but added, "Well you know I wrote a bunch more good songs after that record, too."

"I know you have, buddy," I told him. "I've heard them all." But you have to know which album is my favorite, even if I don't allow myself to listen to it.

And as I can't have Jamie or my father anymore, I also won't have Warren Zevon: He died last year. I'd heard he had cancer, so it wasn't a surprise, but it still hit me like a gut-punch. I went out that day and through a veil of tears bought every fucking CD of his that they had at Tower Records. I went outside, then, and started passing them out to strangers out on the boulevard.

His last album ended up being one of the best; achingly beautiful and poignant, a final message from a man who knew the end was nigh, but kept on being himself anyway—he knew who he was, and he never forgot it. You've got to respect that.

Being so close to the beach right now is tough, and I think my brother must sense that. Jenkins says, "What's going through that mind of yours right now? Thinking about old times?"

"My heart got a little broken in this neck of the woods once, you know."

"But everything worked out in the end."

I try to smile. I start to say, yeah, for me. But I don't.

●

Now Jenkins is at the microphone making his hellfire-and-brimstone rallying cry to the troops. Hollings, red-faced, hoots along with the crowd at some arcane political joke I don't get, being ill-interested as I am in all things political—but especially South Carolina political. Like another world to me, now, this place. When I left, finally, I left for keeps. Had to— felt like that was the only way to stay sane. If I thought I needed a reason to escape before, after Myrtle Beach, I had no other choice.

Big stomachs become filled with bog and barbecue and iced tea so sweet it tastes like maple syrup. The speech is made; the crowd, mostly partisan in composition, cheers for my brother in a sustained, robust fashion. I'm proud of him, so proud.

"But now you've heard enough out of me. Besides, I think there's someone here to whom you would probably rather listen." Jenkins, gesturing in my direction. "Someone whose voice you might recognize. Ray-Ray?"

Thunderous applause. I approach the microphone, shaking hands and waving like one of the pols.

"We might ought to run this young man instead of you, Governor," Hollings says with a twinkle in his eye. "He's mighty popular."

I laugh and shake my head. "An actor? No way, Senator. No way." Then I give him a wink and turn to the crowd. *"Well,"* I say in my best Ronnie Reagan, "it's been done before, but that's a matter of national security, and I can't discuss that right now. We begin bombing in five minutes. Mommy? Is it time for my astrology reading?"

The crowd breaks up; I take little bow.

"Anything you want to say to these people, Ray?"

I scan the mass of faces regarding me, and try to think of what voice to use, but all I can do is count the moments when I can get back in the car and be myself again.

So I do a few bits, run through some old routines, imitate Strom Thurmond and Bill Clinton and George W and finally Hollings himself, tailoring the act to the room, so to speak. I talk in my own voice, then, about what a fine Senator my brother will make. I mention Daddy, and how much it all means to him and Mother, and the stump meeting is over. To a last round of applause, I bid them *adieu* with one last, *"Tank you veddy much,"* just like when I was back in the dunking booth.

As we press the flesh and pose for pictures, Jenkins wonders how long I'm staying. He asks whether or not he should call the Mansion and tell them to expect one more for breakfast tomorrow.

"No," I reply as a little girl runs up to me and requests her favorite character, so I give her thirty seconds of Biggles, my six-toed sarcastic tomcat from the TV show.

She runs back to her father with stars in her eyes. "He sounded just like him," I hear her exclaim. "Oh, Daddy, he sounded just like Biggles!"

"Where will you stay, then?"

"Probably ride out to the beach. Take a day or two for myself. Haven't done that in a long time."

"Good for you. But—here?"

"Maybe it will turn out better this time."

"Myrtle Beach has changed since the old days, you know. You might not recognize it."

"That's not all bad." But I'm not as sure as I try to sound.

I PULL onto 501 and head east. As I maneuver through the heavy traffic—the season is starting to get into swing—I look in the review mirror to see faces: Jamie and Sheila and Paco and Carl Wilson and my Dad, one after the other, their once-shining eyes melding and melting and fading away into the receding past. I pass through Conway and over the Atlantic Intra-coastal Waterway, and soon I see what Jenkins meant: I am stunned at the growth, the condo towers, the sprawl of entertainments. The one-time 'redneck riviera' has come into its own.

I check into the Yachtsman, which now features a slender tower of glass in between the old condo buildings. I look forward to the grits at the Olympic Flame tomorrow morning, which by all measures looks no different.

I sit by myself on the small balcony, watching the modest surf; the beach a dozen floors below is well crowded with late spring vacationers.

Alone again, naturally.

I think about Sheila; I allow myself to realize she would be in her seventies, now—that she might not even be alive anymore. I glance a half-mile down the beach, toward the old Grand Strand Family Motel, but all I can see are other towers like the one in which I now sit.

At least the Pavilion a few blocks up Ocean Boulevard is still going strong. Tomorrow morning I'll have to get a sack of warm caramel corn and see if they still have a dunking booth. Maybe listen to the Baden Band Organ one more time.

After a while I stretch and go downstairs to wander onto the 14th Avenue pier, through a restaurant loud with boisterous, happy drinkers and vacationers. I nod at a cute server, pug-nosed and short like Jamie. She gives me a sweet smile as I pass by her on my way outside.

I walk to the end, until I can go no further. I lean against the weathered rail, the smell of salt and freshly-caught fish in my nostrils. A stiff, warm wind rushes at me from places unknown as I stand mute, staring into the opaque green-black of the ocean; its secrets remain as closely held as my own. It is getting late. I stand alone on the pier—me and the beach and the wind on my face.

AFTERWORD

(2007)

While I have taken reasonable pains to ensure the accuracy of this story's milieu and the cultural references of the period, I did in fact take a few liberties—historical accuracy sacrificed in the name of dramatic license must surely be the most common of authorial sins, but hopefully one that is pardonable. Could you have *really* seen the roller coaster while dining down the block at Mammy's Kitchen? We'll never know.

A few other items of note: I don't know how or by whom the Myrtle Beach Pavilion was managed in the era of this story; since the beginnings of the recently closed amusement park were as a traveling carnival, I couldn't help but imagine some eccentric, ethnic character like Mr. Pugliesi running the place, and so in this universe, he does just that. Other details, too, are fudged a bit about the neighborhood—hey, it was a long time ago.

Tourists with long memories (and residents of the area) who may have frequented Huntington Beach State Park will note that the Atalaya mansion circa 1978 was not the stripped-to-the-bricks structure of today as I describe it in Chapter 8; my memories of a visit there during the seventies is that of the building still having rooms with doors, sheetrock walls, etc. (My father, ever the contrarian, opened a door that said *Do Not Open* only to observe several annoyed individuals sitting on a sofa watching television, so I assume that some parts of Atalaya may have still been in use at the time.) A recent excursion to the mansion I made with my wife, on an atmospheric and lonesome morning much like the one that Ray and Jamie experience together, provides the setting for their final sweet moment more in the service of symbolic, rather than historical value.

As for the numerous pop culture references, a few are anachronistic, but only just-so: Ray's oblique reference to the new "Pete Townshend anthem" is flat-out wrong: The Who album *Who Are You* was not released until August of 1978. Ray's mention of Robin Williams and his manic persona is another cheat: *Mork & Mindy* didn't show up on TV screens until that autumn. Likewise, Ray could possibly have been aware of Andy Kaufman's "Foreign Man" character, but it is worth noting that the television series *Taxi* did not premier until September 12, 1978, and Kaufman's schtick was not as widely known until after the show became a hit.

Ray and his roommate Chris would have had plenty of time, however, to absorb and enjoy Warren Zevon's excellent album *Excitable Boy*; it was released in January that year, and went on to be certified gold by June (and later platinum in 1997). Critically acclaimed (as Ray notes to Jamie), Zevon would be named by *Rolling Stone* magazine as one of the most important new songwriters to emerge in the 1970's. In his unfortunate absence at this far remove of 2007, Zevon's musicianship and irascible wit are as missed as ever—but the work will live on, the end result about which all artists dream for their efforts.

I started this novel several years ago, and while in the interim I finished two other, much more complicated works, it was to *King's Highway* my thoughts often returned. In the summer of 2006 I began making the big push to finish this story, because when I heard that the Pavilion would be closing at the end of the season—forever—I knew the time had come to finally complete the project. I hope you enjoyed reading it as much as I did writing it.

AFTERWORD

(2018)

Ah, ten years—it went by as if in a dream. An all-but happy one.

Sure, tragedies came my way. Life-rending mega-events like the protracted illness and death of my mom. Still I persevered through the writing, the shopping of the work, the promotion of the Red Letter Press edition of this novel and my sophomore effort *Fellow Traveler*, which came courtesy the all-around tireless arts advocates at Muddy Ford Press.

As the years passed and other book deals failed to fluoresce in a manner productive, it fell to this writer, as it does to many nowadays, to publish myself. As such, 2016 saw the founding of Mind Harvest Press, which now has a number of efforts under its belt. By the time of this new, updated edition of *King's Highway* goes on sale, this author's magnum opus, the *Dixiana* series, will have begun emerging and represent the peak event in the Edgewater County series kicked off in 2007 by this small coming-of-age novel set in a favorite locale from my childhood.

Yeah—I always knew I'd not only write a book like this, but it would hit certain narrative beats, and here we are. Not only that, but readers through the last decade have responded with many kind words, including one gentleman who felt prompted by the story to revisit an estranged son, which he said he might not have done were it not for reading my little Myrtle Beach story. "Your book changed my life," he said. No higher compliment could this author imagine—can you?

While my ongoing ambition has long eclipsed the modest aims of this short novel, knowing I created emotional responses in human beings at remote distances through my work in the first published effort remains one of the highlights of my adult life. As Ray Bradbury, the kind of writer Ray-Ray DeKalb would surely have read, would put it, there's no greater reward than hearing from a reader who says you've written a fine, compelling story. Lots of readers have told me that now about *King's Highway*. Here's hoping you may now count yourself among that group. Thanks for taking the ride with me one last time at the old Pavilion.

—James D. McCallister
    September 2018

ABOUT THE AUTHOR

James D. McCallister is the author of ten novels, two short story collections and numerous pieces of short fiction, creative nonfiction, and academic writing. A lifelong South Carolinian, he resides in West Columbia with his wife and beloved brood of cats, muses all.

CONTACT JAMES D McCALLISTER:
www.jamesdmccallister.com
jamesdmccallister@gmail.com

THE EDGEWATER COUNTY SERIES

RETURN TO
EDGEWATER COUNTY
in

Fellow Traveler
Let the Glory Pass Away
The Year They Canceled Christmas
Dogs of Parsons Hollow

and

DIXIANA (2019)
DOWN IN DIXIANA (2019)
DIXIANA DARLING (2020)
RECONSTRUCTION OF THE FABLES (2021)
MANSION OF HIGH GHOSTS (2021)
WANDO (2022)

Mind Harvest Press
COLUMBIA, SC

www.jamesdmccallister.com

www.ingramcontent.com/pod-product-compliance
Lightning Source LLC
Chambersburg PA
CBHW060603190726

48283CB00003B/1135